To Kayle,
I hope you enjoy
book as much as I enjoyed
writing it.
Ann Chandler

Hannah's Story

Ann S. Chandler

Hannah's Story

Copyright 2013® by Ann S. Chandler

All rights reserved. This book may not be reproduced by any means either in whole or in parts, excluding passages for the purpose of magazine or newspaper reviews, without the written consent of the publisher or the author.

ISBN 978-0-9802247-3-3

Library of Congress 2012946920

First Edition, 2013

Edited by Samuel W. Hopkins. Jr.

Design and Layout by Christine D. Kjosa

Published by the SamPat Press

Printed in the United States of America
by Lightning Source, Inc.

Correspondence and publication requests contact:
SamPat Press
1027 Timothy
Jacksonville, TX 75766
(903) 586-4488
http://sampatpress.com/

*This book is dedicated to all who have helped and encouraged me,
Especially to those whom I love most in the world:
David and Suzanne, Casey and Lesley, and my precious
Elle and Rex.*

Hannah's Story
A Journal for Grandma

Part 1 ....Going to Texas
Entries 1-32

Part 2..................Indian Territory
Entries 33-67

Part 3..................Back to the Beginning
Entries 68-81

Part One
Going to Texas

Entry 1

I guess I need to write in my journal. It's been several days since the bad things happened and all I've done is cry. But I can't cry anymore.

My grandmother gave me this journal before we left Alabama and told me that I should write in it every day -- that I should write down what happens because I am the official family historian. Well, that doesn't make sense. History is big things like battles. Maybe what I heard was a battle. Anyway, history is big things and what we do every day is just everyday, but my grandmother said that's what history is made of. So, I'm going to tell my story, and maybe it'll all make sense some day.

I'll start back before we left home. Home was a farm in Talladega County, Alabama. Daddy decided that we needed to move west. I was eight years old. I was born on September 2, 1828, but we left before my birthday. It was August 1837 when we left and it was just mother and daddy and my older sister, Lizzie, my two brothers, Eli and Levi and me. I am Hannah Grace Williams. A whole bunch of people, mostly families, joined us, or we joined them. All the families lined their wagons up. I don't know how they decided who would be first and who would be next, and all that. Some people had two big wagons, one full of furniture and the other one to ride in and sleep in. Some people (always the men and boys) slept on the ground under their wagons. At night we would make a big circle out of the wagons and put the horses and mules and other livestock in the middle of the circle. It was such a big circle that the men would build a fire in the very middle and the women would cook supper there for their families. While the mothers cooked supper, the children would play and explore where we were. We could never get out of sight of the wagons though and could never play alone. We knew there were black bears around – and we didn't know what else.

My Granny Williams couldn't come along because she has the "room-uh-tiz" so bad. She said the trip would be too hard on an old lady. Well, I guess room-uh-tiz is something that you catch from your relatives because my daddy has it too. That is why his two brothers came along with us. They are Elbert and Kias (his real name is Barakias, but we call him "Kias"). He's in love with my Aunt Elizabeth. That's kinda confusing because Elizabeth is only 18 years old and she is my aunt. My big sister is also named Elizabeth, but she is 15 years old. I'm talking about now, not when we left Alabama.

What I started to say about room-uh-tiz is that Daddy can't always work out in the fields, so his brothers work in his place when he feels bad and that's why they went with us, that and also the thing about Kias and Elizabeth being in love.

We got all our stuff into two wagons; we threw a lot of stuff away and we gave a lot of stuff to other people and just left a lot of stuff back home. We had furniture in one wagon, and we had all sorts of foodstuffs in the other and that's where we rode when we were not walking. Just before we left Granny Williams gave me the journal and told me to bring them (she said there would be a lot) back to her when I come back to Alabama. I don't know if I will ever get back now, but I'm going to try to do what she said.

Entry 2

So we started to the West; I really didn't know what that meant at the time, but anyway, I was eight years old and I had my dolly and I still have my dolly. And my grandmother gave me this little book and it didn't have any writing in it. It was just blank pages and she said it was a journal and I had to keep it and write down every thing that happens from now on forever. We talked about that and she told me I didn't have to tell everything – like every time I get a drink of water and things like that, but at night before I go to bed I am supposed to think back over the day and write down what I remember about that day. Then when I take it back to her in Alabama, she will know everything that happened.

Okay, so our family – and we are the Williams -- got together with my grandparents. Their name is Killough. This my mother's family, not Granny Williams, who is Daddy's mother, and my aunts, my uncles, their kids, and my little baby cousin, and his little dog and we all started on this trip to the West to a new home. There were about 30 of us in our family and we joined some other wagons and pretty soon it was a pretty big group. We rode, and we rode, and we rode. Some days I walked and some days I rode in the wagon. Sometimes it was fun and sometimes it was just boring. The most fun was when they let me ride up on one of the mules pulling one of our wagons. There were two mules pulling each of our wagons and sometimes another little girl who was on the train, but not one of my cousins, and I, would each ride on a mule. We would tell stories, and we would dream about what the new place would be like. We went on for days and forever, it seemed like, and we crossed some big rivers and along the way some other wagons would join us and some of the other wagons would stop somewhere. They would decide that they were going to go in a different direction, or they were just tired. I don't know. The grownups talked about the people who left the wagon train. But I didn't really listen. One other thing we did along the way that was kinda fun was that my sister Elizabeth was our teacher. She had to teach my two brothers, Levi and Eli – their names are alike because they are twins. Elizabeth is 15 and the twins are 12 and I was only 8, but I had my ninth birthday along the way. We were on our journey when September 2 came and I was 9 years old. Let me tell you about my ninth birthday. Every night the wagon train would stop and we would make camp. The girls and women and little kids would sleep in the wagons and the men and big boys would sleep on pallets on the ground.

Anyway, when it was my birthday, Momma and some of the other women – mostly my aunts – made me a birthday cake. I thought you had to have a cook stove like at home to bake a cake, but someone must have told my mother how to make a cake over a campfire. She mixed it up and put it in a real heavy pan that she called a Dutch oven and set the pan on the fire and turned the lid upside down and put red-hot coals in the turned-over lid. It was not the best cake I've ever tasted but it was the first sweet thing we had eaten since we left home – and it was just for me. Of course, everybody had some, but I mean it was made just because it was my birthday. I got some presents, too, but they were just clothes. The cake was the best thing to me.

Anyway, I was going to tell about our own little "school." Elizabeth is real smart and along the way sometimes some of the other children on the wagon train would come to our wagon and Elizabeth would teach all of us. She had to teach pretty hard things because my brothers would not pay attention if it was just baby stuff. So, I learned some geography, especially about the country we were going through, and I studied some stories, especially by William Shakespeare because the boys liked the sword fights and all. We also studied some arithmetic that was really hard for me but the boys liked it and could do it.

Of course we studied the Bible, but that was mostly Momma who told us the Bible stories at night and sometimes Daddy would, too. When I wrote in my journal, Daddy would say that I was learning the 3 R's, but that's not exactly right because only Reading starts with an "R", Writing and Arithmetic just sound kinda like they start that way, but that's what grownups say because I heard some of the other grownups say 3 Rs, too.

Entry 3

Finally we crossed this huge river and that was interesting.

It was the Mississippi River and it was so big. We went way up beside the river for a long way and then we stopped. The men built rafts out of trees they cut down and one by one they would load a wagon on the raft and let it float down the river. There were some men on the raft and they would try to steer it to the far side of the river. Finally, when the raft and the wagon got to the other side, it would be a long way from where it started. There were separate rafts just for people and animals. Daddy said they did that because it was dangerous for the people to ride with the wagons. Then the people from that raft would make camp and wait for the other wagons to cross the river and catch up with them. It took a long time, but it was kinda fun.
After we crossed a couple of more rivers that were not so big, we got to this place called Nacogdoches. It was the fall of 1837 (and I was 9 years old and getting pretty smart from all the things Elizabeth was teaching us) when we got to Nacogdoches, and it was a big town and had stores and everything.

We stayed there for a little while and then we went to the place that would be our new home. There wasn't a town there and no neighbors so it didn't have a name; it was just out in the forest. But the day we got to our new home was Christmas Eve. We didn't have a cabin, but we had a Christmas tree! Daddy and my uncles cut one down and the women popped corn and we put it on threads to decorate the tree. Then the two Elizabeths and some of my girl cousins went out in the woods to find some red berries to put on strings, too. Kias went with us to protect us, but mostly he and Elizabeth (my aunt, not my sister) held hands and acted silly. It was just an excuse for him to be with her. If a wild animal had come along, it would just have eaten us for all the attention he was paying. Anyway, we found berries and a couple of old bird's nests and brought them back to camp.

We had the most fun that night. Some of my aunts cooked and some helped decorate the tree. The men sat around and talked about where they were going to build their cabins – I'll tell you what they decided later – but the most fun and the biggest surprise was next. After we ate, Grandpa Isaac read the Christmas story from the book of Luke in the Bible – then we all got presents!

We (the kids, I mean) didn't expect any presents this year, but Grandpa Isaac said that he saw Santa Claus when we were in Nacogdoches and he told Santa that we were going to be on the frontier and that Santa gave him our presents for Grandpa to deliver for him.

I'm big enough that I don't believe in Santa Claus any more, but I pretended to for the little kid's sake. Momma and I had talked about it and she said Santa Claus was the name for the spirit of love that makes your momma and daddy want to give you something you will like. I really know that the grownups must have gone shopping in Nacogdoches and have hidden the presents until tonight.

There were really good things! We all got hard candy and some kind of toy or clothing that we wanted. I got some ribbons for my hair and a new dress for my doll, Anna. I asked Momma if I was too old to have a doll, and she said, "No" that I should stay a child as long as I could because once I became a grownup, I could never go back to being a child and would have be grown up for the rest of my life.

Now I think all that has changed. I want more than anything in the world to go back to being my momma's little girl, but I don't guess I ever can. I guess Momma was right – you can't go backwards!

Entry 4

I need to write down what Texas (that's where we ended up) is like. Momma says it is just like Eden in the Bible. There is a lot of water and lots of trees and grass and lots and lots of animals. It is hot in the summer, but not as hot as Alabama.

And my grandparents – Isaac and Urcey Killough -- and some of my aunts and uncles and my cousins, we all got there and stayed there a while. The men cut down trees and out of the trees they cut down, they built cabins. After the men talked and planned on Christmas Eve, they got started the next day on the cabins. This is the way our little "village" looked. First, all the men cut down trees and built a cabin for my grandparents and my aunt Elizabeth (she still lives with them). This is the middle cabin and the biggest. Then all Granddaddy and Grandmother's kids cleared land and built their cabins in a circle around their parents.

Isaac, Jr. (we call him Uncle Junior) and Aunt Jane built their cabin directly in front of my grandparents. That's south. Directions are something that I learned on the way here, and I'm really good at it. Daddy says I have a natural sense of direction and that lots of people don't.

Back to our houses. Uncle Allen and his family built to the west of Grandpa and Grandma. Uncle Sam and Aunt Sissy (that's really Samuel and Narcissa) and my little baby cousin Billy live to the east. Aunt Jane and Uncle George (they are the Woods) and their five children have a pretty big cabin sort of southwest of my grandparents. The little "village" took up a lot of space and some of the cabins we couldn't see from the others, but that was the general plan.

Only my uncle Nathaniel and his wife kinda broke away from this plan. They built their cabin across a creek to the south of my Uncle Isaac and Aunt Jane. In all, there were seven cabins, with my grandparents in the middle.

We (Owen and Polly Williams and their four kids – including me – and Daddy's two brothers) lived farthest to the north. I'll draw a picture in my journal to show what it looked like.

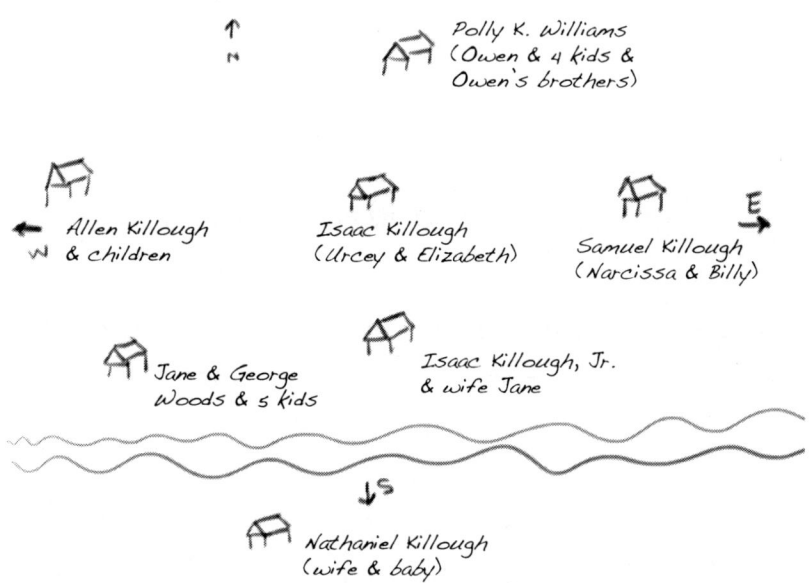

Back to the story: Where they had cut down the trees, they would clear the land and plant crops. And it was really good. Things were o.k. for a while. My grandmother (Killough) gave me a new journal because I had nearly filled up my first one. So she gave me another one and I started it.

Entry 5

I don't know where my first journal is. I don't even know where my grandmother is. I don't know where my parents are. But, anyway, I am not going to think about that because it makes me so sad that I can't stand it.

O.k., so we were at our new home and all my relatives were close by and we planted our crops and it was spring of 1838 and everything was o.k., except I heard Daddy talking to some of the other men – my uncles and my granddaddy.

They were talking about there being some Indian unrest. I don't know what "unrest" means, but anyway our crops were planted but everybody just left them and our houses and all. We went back to Nacogdoches. I don't know how to spell it, but I did learn how to say it. It took us all of one whole day and part of another to get there because of the slow wagons. Daddy said that on a good horse, a man could make it in a single day.

It was a big town and a lot of people lived there. So, we stayed there all summer. Usually you don't go to school in the summer, but my sister Elizabeth taught us every day and we were really getting smart. I always called my sister Lizzie and my aunt Elizabeth, but now for some reason, I want to spell out my sister's name. It just kinda feels like she deserves it so I use her real name.

By the time it was time to harvest the crops, Daddy said he had gotten reports that it was o.k. to go back and get our crops, and then we would move back to Nacogdoches because we would be safer. So, we went on back to our home, to our cabins and there still weren't any other people living there except some Indians nearby, but we never saw them, I just heard my daddy and my uncles talking about them.

We went back so the men could harvest the corn. The women were canning things to put up to take with us to our new home in Nacogdoches. And, one day, and this was the bad day — the worst day of my whole life — my mother told me to take my basket and to go pick grapes. She said so that I wouldn't get my dress all stained with grape juice, I had to put this big apron on. It covered up the whole skirt of my dress and it hung down. It had two big pockets in it. So, I put my doll, in one pocket (my doll's name is Anna) and I put my journal -- and it was a new journal -- in my other pocket. It didn't have anything written in it except my name, and my age and my birthday. Oh, I won't know when it's my birthday! I'm not going to let me think about that because I'll just start crying again.

So I put my journal and pencil in the other pocket and I carried the basket. I went a ways to where the road is. It's a little ways north from our house and it's an old, old, old road. My daddy called it a "trace," but it's really a road, but it's deep. Daddy said the road was real deep because wagons and animals and people had used it for so long that it wore it down. The grapes grew on the side of this trace/road thing, so I started picking grapes and I kept picking and picking and I didn't realize it, but I was going farther and farther away from my house. That was o.k. because I knew how to get back home. But then I heard this horrible noise.

Entry 6

I heard horses running, and I heard yelling and I heard shooting. I have never been so scared in my life. I didn't know what to do, so I climbed into the middle of this big grape vine. It was kinda scratchy, but I climbed into it and hid. I stayed there a long time and I was shaking and crying and I was trying to be quiet. Then pretty soon – or at least some time had passed – the noise all stopped. And I kept thinking should I go back home – maybe I should. I didn't know and there wasn't any grownup around to tell me what to do. Even though I'm smart, I'm still just a kid and I need a grown-up to tell me what to do sometimes.

Then I heard some horses coming down this road, this trace. And I peeked out and it was three Indians and they were going toward my house. So, I waited, and I didn't know what that meant and I didn't know what to do so I just waited and I just hugged and I rocked my doll and that's all I could do. And I ate some grapes, too. After a while I heard horses again, and it was the same three Indians; they were coming back from the direction of my house and nobody was with them. So, I don't know what they did there.

Anyway, they must have seen me back in the grapevine because they stopped and one of them pulled me out of the grapevine. And I kicked and I screamed, and I fought but he was real strong and no one came to help me. He didn't speak my language at all and I don't speak Indian, but he kept saying, "Dog Shoot, Dog Shoot." At first I thought, is he shooting dogs? Does he want to shoot a dog? I don't have a dog. My little cousin Billy has a little fiest dog, but what's "Dog Shoot" mean? Then when I quit crying enough, he started beating on his chest, and every time he would hit his chest, he would say, "Dog Shoot, Dog Shoot." I finally figured that his name was Dog Shoot. Indians have funny names.

I couldn't do anything to help it, but this Indian put me on his horse in front of him and he and the other two Indians kept talking in Indian and we rode off and all the time he had his arm around me real tight and I couldn't move at all. And I lost my basket with the grapes in it. But I didn't lose my doll and I didn't lose my journal. They were in my pockets.

So we rode and we rode and we came to a cabin and it had a great big chimney. The chimney was built out of rocks and it was giant. Another Indian came out of the cabin and it was kinda funny. This Indian must have been the boss and he spoke a little bit of English, but not much. He was able to tell me his name was the Bench. I said, "The Bench?" and I acted like I was going to sit down and he said "Bench, Bench," and he nodded his head. His name must be Bench, so I started calling him Mr. Bench.

Mr. Bench was probably about as old as my daddy. His cabin was very much like a cabin we would live in but it was bigger. In fact, the circle of cabins was just like our cabins with Mr. Bench's in the middle and three other little cabins around it. Only at this place, the stream was to the north instead of to the south like it was at our little village.

Inside the cabin (I learned this later) Mr. Bench lived and I guess he had three wives – I don't know – that's confusing to me. Some little kids lived there too. They all lived inside. That's where they let me live too. Outside in a circle, there were all these little cabins and these Indian men lived in them with their families. The way the cabins were built with Mr. Bench's in the middle let me know that he was the chief, just like my granddaddy with his cabin in the center was the chief of our little "tribe." That's kinda funny to think about. But where my granddaddy is old, Mr. Bench was not, just grownup like Daddy.

Entry 7

That first night I learned everybody's name. I remembered how Dog Shoot had taught me his name so I did the same thing. I would go to one person and say, "My name is Hannah, what's your name?" After I had done this a couple of times, the Indians learned to say, "My name is," and whatever their name was.

Now I didn't write in my journal that day. I have not written in about a week. I was too sad. Anyway, during the daytime the men would go and do things that men do. Some of them worked in the fields, but not many. They harvested the stuff that was grown, but the women did most of the planting. They also killed animals for the women to save and to cook. There was a smokehouse and a little creek nearby that had really cold water in it.

I didn't know at first; it took me probably a week to figure out, but somebody was with me all the time. I guess they were afraid I would run away or something. For that first week I didn't do anything. I just cried a lot and played with my doll. Then after about a week, Mr. Bench, who didn't know much English, but he could make himself understood by using words and hand signs and grunting and stuff like that, -- he said something about somebody coming.

Anyway, this very, very, very old man showed up. He had all these other Indians with him. He could speak English pretty well and he came just to see me! We visited a while and he told me that he was the chief, the big chief. He said his name was Duwali, but that they called him the Bowl, like a bowl that you eat out of. I asked him what about my family and he said, "They're all gone." So, I cried a while and he let me sit on his lap and he put his arms around me and he just let me cry. And after a while, when I finished crying, he put me back on the ground and said he would be back soon.

Then he and his Indians rode away. A couple of days later a couple of the Indians who had been with Mr. Duwali came back. They talked to Mr. Bench for a long time and they watched me a lot. I don't know what that was all about, but they left and came back again and did the same thing again – talking to Mr. Bench and watching me. That night Mr. Bench wanted to talk to me outside the cabin. We walked down to the creek and he said that the Big Chief (Duwali) would be back the next day and that he had decided that he wanted to make me a member of the Cherokee tribe. I asked why and how that was possible. Mr. Bench said that Mr. Duwali could do anything he wants to and that apparently he thinks that he can protect me better if I am a member of his "family" and that I am important to the Cherokees because I am teaching them how to talk American.

Finally Mr. Bench said that Mr. Duwali plans to adopt me. Well, I know what that means because a woman back in my hometown in Alabama had a boy that she had adopted. I asked Mr. Bench what about my own family, and he looked at me funny and said that if Duwali wanted something, he got it. I take that to mean that I don't have any say in the matter.

Anyway, I didn't know how I was supposed to get ready, so the next morning I combed my hair and I put my doll in my pocket and I put my journal in my other pocket. I still had my big apron – in fact, all the clothes I had were the ones I had been wearing the day Dog Shoot got me out of the grapevine. I'll say it that way and maybe I won't cry.

Mr. Duwali got here about dinner time. The Indians built a big fire out in the yard and everything. It was getting dark by that time. It was either late in October or early in November so it was a little cool, but it wasn't cold. So, all these Indian men danced around this fire and they hooted and hollered and made noises, kinda like singing.

They said all these words in Indian and I had to come and stand in front of Mr. Duwali and I guess that was the adoption. It went on for a while and they all talked in Indian words.

Then it was over.

Entry 8

In a way I did not want to be adopted—it felt like I was not being a good granddaughter to my real grandparents, but after I thought about it, it seemed ok, one, because my grandfather Williams was dead, so Duwali was just kinda standing in for him, and two, I figured that because Duwali is such a big chief, maybe being his granddaughter would help me. One thing I could never be is Mr. Bench's daughter because I have a daddy of my own and that's that!

Mr. Duwali and I talked for a long time after the Indians made me his granddaughter and he asked me what I wanted to do, and I told him I wanted to go home and see my parents and my family, and he just shook his head and said, "They're all gone. They're all gone." I said, "Do you know where they went?" He shook his head like he was sad and said, "No, they're all gone." Then I cried a little more and my new grandfather just let me.

Then he asked me to tell him about me, so I told him about Alabama and I told him about my Granny Williams and that he would like her because she was such a nice lady. And I showed him my journal. It only had about one day written in it. I had not written in it in a long time, and he was real impressed that I could read and could write.

He said that my job was to do exactly what my Granny said, to keep writing down what happened and he would make sure that I always would have plenty of paper and plenty of pencils. And my job in his tribe was to teach the children English – how to speak it, how to read it, and how to write it. He said, "Don't worry about learning Indian language." He said, "You'll pick that up." That's the way he said it, "You'll pick that up." I'm not sure exactly what that means, but I guess it means that I won't have a teacher like Elizabeth was. I'll just have to learn Indian on my own.

But he said that every day he wanted me to be the teacher, and he wanted me to teach the little children at the cabin. He said that was the most important job I could do. I said, "O.K."

Entry 9

So that's what I started doing the very next day. Apparently Duwali is the big chief, and Mr. Bench is a little chief because Mr. Duwali talked to Mr. Bench in Indian for a long time and the next day Mr. Duwali left with all the Indians that travel with him. Then Mr. Bench found -- but I don't know where -- some paper and some pencils and he let me use part of the big cabin like a school room.

Some of the students were younger than I am and some of them were older and the big kids still had to do their chores, but every morning and every evening for about an hour, I would teach them how to speak English. I would point to something and I would say what it was in English and they would repeat it. They were learning pretty fast. We weren't going to get down to reading and writing for a while. First I was just going to have them learn the words.

At first Chooch would not try to learn. Chooch is Mr. Bench's son, so Mr. Bench took him outside and I guess he talked to him or something. I was crying, but I tried not to show it. When they came back in Chooch was o.k. but Mr. Bench just looked at me kinda funny. What he did not know and I couldn't talk enough Indian to tell him was that nearly the same thing happened on the way from Alabama. When Elizabeth was first starting to teach us my brother Eli said that he wouldn't let Elizabeth teach him, that he was too big and she was just a girl. My daddy took him outside the wagon and wore him out. From then on the lessons were o.k.

When Chooch did the same thing, it just made me so sad for my family – even my brothers – that I couldn't help crying.

So, we did that for a while. Oh, one other thing I asked Mr. Bench, I said, "Mr. Bench, do you know what day it is." He asked me why and I said, "Well, I'm saddest because I don't have my parents here with me anymore, but I'm second saddest because I don't know what day it is. I won't know when it's Christmas"

He just looked at me because he didn't know what that meant – I said, "I won't know when it's my birthday, I won't know anything about the time." He just kinda laughed and he said, "The time is what it is. Man calls it different days, but those days are made by man." Then he said he would find out what day it is and he tell me what the day is. "You can keep up with it." I said, "O.K."

So, it was several days and Mr. Bench had been somewhere, and when he got back he told me the day and at that time it was in November, so I drew a calendar because I knew the thing people used to say about 30 days hath September, April, June, and November. So I knew that November had 30 days and when he told me the day it was in November, I drew a calendar like the one we had on the wall in my family cabin. I don't know if it is Sunday or Wednesday, or whatever, I'll just take Mr. Bench's word what day it is – I don't understand "man-made" that the time is what it is. Anyway, when he told me what day it was, I worked and worked and worked to figure it out. I know it was October 5 when the horrible thing happened at my home and I marked all that down after I finally figured it out.

Anyway, I think I got the day of the week figured out. I'm not sure I'm right, but I drew a calendar for October and then I drew a new calendar for November on some of my new paper. So every night before I went to bed, I would write in my journal and then I would draw an "x" across the little square for that day. So if I'm here for that long, I'll know when it is my birthday, if nothing else.

I talked a whole lot to Anna, my little doll, and I played with the dogs – there were a lot of dogs around, and I taught the school and that's what I did every day for a long, long time.

Entry 10

Writing in my journal is kinda funny. Every night that I write, I begin writing to Granny Williams, but before I have written much, it's like I am writing to the journal. It's kinda like writing a letter and it feels like I am writing "Dear Journal" just like the journal is a person. I don't really understand it and don't have anyone to talk to about it – or about anything!

It isn't my family, and I still miss them horribly and I still cry all the time for them, but I guess it's the best I can do right now.

Oh, I forgot to tell how the people treated me and it's all because of my new granddaddy, Duwali. After we went through that adoption thing, everybody was so nice to me. They did things for me and they rushed around and they acted like I was really somebody important. They liked me a lot better. That was o.k., too. I tried not to take advantage, my momma would have said, of the situation, but it sure was hard, but that's the way things went on for a long time.

The days went by, with every day at Mr. Bench's just about the same and still it was interesting. I watched my calendar on the wall and thought a lot about Christmas. I love Christmas – maybe even better than my birthday. After all, it is Baby Jesus' birthday and everybody gets presents. The Indians don't know anything about Christmas or even about Baby Jesus, but since I'm their teacher, maybe I can teach them that.

I talk to Mr. Bench sometimes and I am trying to tell him what Christmas is and all about presents and things. It's easier to explain about presents than to try to tell him about the spirit of love like my momma told me — but Indians don't know anything about Santa Claus. I just realized that if I don't tell them, they may never know. That makes my teaching feel kinda important. It makes me think that I need to do more than just teach the Indians how to talk. I may be just a kid, but I know a lot of things that even the grown-up Indians don't know.

Since there isn't a town and there isn't anything to buy anybody for Christmas, I guess I will just have to make presents for everybody myself.

I need to write down everyone's name so I can let Granny Williams know who I lived with. The oldest woman living in the cabin is Sookie. She has one boy named Chooch (he's about 15 years old) and a little girl about six years old named Sally. The other two women are Wali and Quatie. Wali has a little girl named Wakie, who is about four or five years old. The youngest woman, Quatie has a little bitty baby named Quatsie. So, in the cabin were Mr. Bench, his three wives and his son and three little girls and me.

Sookie is the kindest to me. She is trying really hard to learn to speak English and she shows me how to cook things and stuff like that. Wali and Quatie are both nice, but since they have little kids to take care of, they don't have as much time for me as Sookie does. She is sort of the senior wife and she only has the boy and he is nearly grown and one little girl, and she likes me.

Out in the yard were three little cabins with the rest of the Indians in them. My own Indian (and I'll tell you why I say that later) was Dog Shoot, but he didn't have a wife. He was nearly as old as Mr. Bench, but maybe not exactly. The other two Indian men each had wives and children. They don't take part in the evening lessons though. The little children show up every morning for the little kids lessons but at night they stay in their own cabins.

I call Dog Shoot "my" Indian because he "rescued" me on the day of the battle (I don't know what else to call it), and at first he kept an eye on me. Probably Mr. Bench told him to watch me so that I wouldn't run away, but I didn't have anywhere to run. He was always kind to me and I guess I got to like him o.k.

Entry 11

Let me tell you about the school lessons. In the morning, after we (I helped) had done the morning chores, I would take the younger children and teach them.

I say "take" because when it was a pretty day, we would have our lessons outside. That made it easier to teach them words for colors and for things that we could see outside.

The ones I taught in the morning are Sally, Wakie and some of the children from the little cabins out in the yard. I never did get their names straight because except for Mr. Bench's family and Dog Shoot, they won't talk to me, but anyway, I called the children I teach in the morning Jane and Polly and Noah. Those were names I knew because Jane was my aunt, Polly was my mother's name and Noah was a cousin's name. There were two other boys beside Chooch who came to the cabin at night for lessons, but their parents didn't come with them. The Indians don't have as many children as the Killoughs had, but I don't know why. We studied every day either in the cabin if it was rainy or cold or outside if it was pretty.

After we had all eaten supper, I would hold lessons again inside the cabin for Chooch and the two big boys. Mr. Bench, his wives, and Dog Shoot would sit around and listen. They were learning English too, and I guess that's what Duwali meant when he said something about "picking up" the language. He was talking about me learning a little Cherokee (that's the kind of Indians they were), but that is what was happening with some of the Indians. They were "picking up" a little English.

Something else that you, Granny, will want to know is what the Indians wear and how they look. Well, they look like you and me and they wear clothes like we do. When Elizabeth was teaching us on the way to Texas, she told about Indians and they were "red-skins" and wore deerskin clothes and shot arrows. Well, maybe some Indians are like that, but the Cherokee are not. The only thing different about them and me is that I have yellow hair and none of them do. Some have red hair, but most have black or dark brown hair. As far as being "a red skin," when I'm out in the sun too long, I get redder than they ever do.

Something that I'm not sure I understand is that every time I leave the cabin, I have to wear a bonnet. Granny Williams and Granny Killough both wore bonnets every time they went out, but the kids at home never did. I'm not sure about Mr. Bench wanting to keep my skin white, which is why my grannies wore bonnets, but if I start to leave the cabin and forget my bonnet, Dog Shoot or one of the women will remind me and make me put it on. Well, that's a little strange, but I guess I can stand it.

Entry 12

As I said earlier, it was getting on toward Christmas and I wanted to have a present for everyone, so I had to make them. I tried and tried and could kinda remember how to make paper dolls, so I made one for each of the girls. I'm so glad that you taught me to knit and crochet, Granny. I saved threads from things that the women were making and I knitted headscarves for them. They weren't very good or very big, but I didn't have as much time to work on them as I would like to. That left the men and boys.

I worried and worried about this. It seems like when I lived with my family, Mother would get money from Daddy and we would buy presents for the other children and the women, too, but Christmas was always mostly for kids. I never thought about money. Everybody who had ever looked after me must have had money. I never wanted anything that I didn't get – except my family back, and money can't buy that.

At Mr. Bench's the women and bigger kids help make salt. Mr. Bench sold it to other Indians and white people, too, and that must be how he made money.

The way he got the salt was that when it rained, there was a low place that would hold the water. When it dried up (instead of soaking in), the men and sometimes the women would cut out thin slices of the dirt. Then the women would boil it in water in one of the big black pots in the yard.

Then they let the water cool in the pot. The dirt, grass, moss, and stuff like that would sink to the bottom. Then they would pour just the water off. It tasted salty, but it wasn't clean yet. Then they would cook it again and drain off the top. After a while, the water was real salty and it was pretty clean. Then they would let the water dry up and what was left in the bottom was salt. Mr. Bench took this and sold it. They let me help a little and I watched what they did. That's how I know how to make salt.

The Indians don't need much. The men hunted and fished and the women would dry the meat that they killed or caught and the salt was used to cure the meat and to buy things like cloth for the women to make clothes with.

The women were the hardest working people in the whole family. The men helped make the salt when they were not out hunting or fishing. The women did everything. The good thing about that is that at night I was so tired that I fell asleep and didn't even have any dreams.

Back to my Christmas presents. I don't know how much money Mr. Bench has and I don't want to ask him for any, and I don't have a store to go to anyway. So, I needed to think of something I could make him that wouldn't cost money. Well, I did have plenty of paper and pencils – we used them in the classroom – so I decided to draw a picture for Mr. Bench. It really did turn out pretty good.

I found a spot outside where I could see the cabin and where it looked good. So, I drew him a picture of his cabin. I made it look prettier than it really is. I didn't put all the junk out in the yard – just the cabin with the big stone chimney and the forest behind it. I didn't have any colors for the picture, so it was just pencil, but it really looked pretty good. Then I made a frame around the picture from twigs I found around the cabins.

That just left the boys. They were the hardest! I made

really pretty balls for the little boys out of clay that I dug out of the creek and dried. I looked for a long time to find just the prettiest colors. The balls are hard and if the little boys throw them and get hit, it will hurt, but the Indians are really good at things like throwing and running and stuff like that, so I guess they will just have to be sure to catch the balls that they throw. Either that or get out of the way.

After I thought about it and thought about it, I decided that I could make the big boys fishing sticks. All the men and boys go over to the river or down to the big creek when they have time and fish and bring the fish back for the women to cure in the smokehouse and we have them to eat when we want them. So, I found a little tree that has great big long thorns on it and pulled some of the thorns off.

Then I looked all around and found some pretty bird feathers. Then I found a couple of long, straight sticks. Sookie gave me some pieces of string (I think it is made out of something about a deer) and I tied the thorns and the feathers on the end of a stick. When the men go fishing, they put the end of their fishing stick in the water and swish it back and forth and it makes a little noise and the fish must think it is a bug or something to eat because they bite at the feathers and sometimes the thorn gets stuck in their mouths and the Indians pull them in. The boys already had some fishing sticks, but now they will each have a new one all their own.

Entry 13

When it got to be Christmas, I tried my best to tell the Indians what it was all about. Only Mr. Bench understands enough English to understand what I'm talking about. He was interested in Baby Jesus and he seemed to understand that I really wanted to have presents for Christmas. So he surprised me!

Maybe because it is his cabin, he always knows everything that is happening in it. He knew that I was making presents and he went out and bought some presents for me! He gave me a Bible and a satchel. The satchel is big enough that I can put the Bible, my journals (I am on the second one since I lost the others) and all the pencils and papers for my school classes inside it.

This Christmas was fun. My Granny Williams always said, "It is better to give than to receive," and I guess I am beginning to understand what she meant. It was so nice to surprise the children with their gifts and the women in the cabin acted like they really liked their scarves, but the best thing was the picture that I made for Mr. Bench. He just looked at it and looked at it, and didn't say anything for a long time. Then he looked me right in the eye and just said, "Thank you," in perfect English.

If I'm still here next Christmas, maybe we can have a Christmas tree. But surely I won't still be here. Maybe I will have been found by then by my daddy or one of my uncles or my brothers or someone and I'll be back with my family. Only I don't want to think about that because it will just make me sad and I'll cry.

I started that very night reading out of the Bible to the Indians in the cabin. They all seemed to like to hear me reading and when I think about it, hearing it will help them say the English words better. So, I plan to read a little to the Indians every night. But after working all day, reading puts the children to sleep and I even read myself to sleep sometimes. That's funny!

Entry 14

One of the things that seems really strange to me is how very quiet the Indians are. Even the young children are quiet, especially when their parents or other adults are around. When I would take the young children outside to have their morning lessons, at first they were silent, but then gradually they started to squeal and run and play like other little children I have been around. When their parents were around, they would put their hands over their mouths to keep from laughing out loud.

One day I saw how the mothers teach the babies not to cry. First of all, the babies are carried around in a sling-like thing so that they are touching their mother's body. This makes it easy to nurse the babies because they are always up against their mother's chest. But today I saw Quatie teach Quatsie how not to cry. It was strange and in a way kinda scary.

The baby started to cry and Quatie put her hand over the baby's mouth and nose so that it was smothering. Then she let go. When the baby had gotten its breath back, it started to cry again. Quatie put her hand over its mouth and nose again. It couldn't make any noise because it couldn't get any air. She repeated this several times until the baby must have figured out that if it cried, it would be smothered.

Quatie is very loving and kind in every other way. I'll watch to see if she does this again, but it does explain why the children are so very quiet. Even the grownups don't talk much. They use gestures and they grunt, but they hardly every say much, even in their own language.

So now, 1838 is over. Lizzie once read us a book (on the way to Texas) that said at the beginning, "It was the best of times; it was the worst of times." I don't remember anything else about the book (I was only about 8 or 9 years old) but everybody in my family, especially Daddy, started saying that.

If Momma, or anybody, asked Daddy what kind of day he had had (you know he has room-uh-tiz real bad), he would always say, "It was the best of times; it was the worst of times."

When I think back over 1838, I want to say, "It was the best of times; it was the worst of times." I really don't want to talk (or write) about what was good and what was bad because I will just make myself sad and I'll cry again. I have grown up a lot, but I'm still a kid and I'm not an Indian – I do talk and cry.

It is winter and many times it is raining or too cold, and we cannot have our morning classes outside. I don't like the days when we have to stay inside. I still have class in the morning and the evening, but the morning class is more like just playing with the little kids.

I talked to Mr. Bench about this and he said that as long as I talked to the little kids in English and made them talk to me in English, they were still learning. He told me not to talk to them in Indian. He knows that I am getting pretty good in Cherokee, but mostly that is just at understanding it. I don't get much chance to talk it.

Mr. Bench is a really smart man. He may even be wise. (I'm reading about that in the New Testament). He's not as wise as my daddy, but he is maybe second. Daddy says having knowledge means knowing things, but being wise means understanding things.

Entry 15

I'm not writing in my journal every day because the days are all pretty much alike. We (the women) all cook, and clean, and sew, and tend to the animals and to the children. We are starting to plant a few things and that takes some time. It seems like we never have any time just to sit and rest. The spring will be busy with crops but when summer gets here we will have more time while the crops are just growing and before the harvest.

One thing that Sookie is teaching me is how to cook. I kinda know how to cook on a wood stove like we had at home. Mostly I would watch Momma and my big sister cook, and they would give me little things to do. Now though I'm old enough to really learn to cook, but we don't have a cook stove. All we have is a great big fireplace. I've only been here since about November so there is always a fire in the fireplace. I don't know what we'll do in the summer when it's hot. Anyway, there is a cut-out place on one side of the fireplace and the Indians use it like an oven. It takes a long time to cook in the oven, but Sookie makes something like cornbread all the time and cooks it in that oven thing.

The Indians grow a lot of corn and we eat it different ways. The funny thing – about white people and Indians – is that we eat some of the same food the animals eat – like corn. There are a couple of cows here so we have milk to drink as well as water. There are also a couple of goats, and of course, the horses. The Indians use the horses for everything except food.

We eat meat just about every day. The men and big boys kill deer and turkeys, and catch fish, and even sometimes (once) they killed one of the cows. But it was old.

The smokehouse has a lot of meat in it. Then there's a place near a great big creek, not our little one to the north. This one is south and a little west of the cabins and it is great big and it runs down into a river. Anyway, there's a cave dug out in the side of the creek bank and we keep potatoes and onions and things in there. We also have a beehive and get honey from it.

We really have good food and I like to cook.

Winter here is not so awfully cold, but it does rain a lot. That makes more work because of the salt job. Oh, well, I wish something interesting would happen, but not more work. I'm pretty tired some of the time, but I'm pretty bored a lot of the time.

Entry 16

I promise I will never again wish for something exciting to happen. I read back over my journal and the last thing I wrote was about our food and about learning to cook. I was writing about that because nothing else was happening. Every day was just the same – chores, school, more chores, and school again, and then reading aloud from the Bible, and then writing in my journal and sleeping. Then the next day was the same. The last thing I wrote was that I was bored and I wished something would happen. Well, I got my wish and now I don't want it.

We got up – it was early spring – March to be exact, and the day started like all the other days. We ate breakfast, straightened up the cabin, started a fire in the yard because it had been raining and we were going to make salt. It wasn't raining, in fact, it was one of the prettiest days so far this year.

Anyway, I took the small children with me and we went to the small creek north of the cabins. The trees were starting to put out new leaves and the grass was starting to grow, so I had planned to teach the children the color green. I had not thought before how many colors of green there are, and I didn't know at first how hard it would be to teach what colors are.

At first we just learned the names of things like bed, chair, floor, wall, and stuff like that. But when I first started teaching colors it was pretty hard. For brown, I would show things like wood and dirt and the kids would say "wood" or "dirt." It took them a long time to get to where they understood that the name of something and its color are not the same.

Finally I think they are starting to understand, and that is because of hair! Everybody understood that we all have hair on our heads, but when I showed them black hair (like some of theirs), and red hair (like Mr. Bench's) and yellow hair (mine) I think they finally understood. So that day we were going to look at green grass, green leaves, and maybe even my eyes because they are green too.

Anyway, we got to the small creek – and it's over a little hill so you can't see the cabins from it and everybody started getting leaves and grass and bringing them to me. We had only been there a little while when I heard horses running fast and then gunshots. All I could think of was the day I was picking grapes and I heard the same sounds. Then, it was like I was frozen, but this time I had five little children with me and I had to take care of them.

What we did was to hide in a little low place with bushes growing all around. It was not as good a hiding place as the grapevines had been, but there were six of us instead of just one little girl. Now I'm older and am bigger and I've gotten a lot more grown up than I was then. But I was still scared!

Entry 17

Anyway, back to the story of what happened. We stayed hidden even after the shooting stopped and we heard the horses running away. When it got quiet, I peeked out from our hiding place and could see a lot of smoke coming from the direction of the cabins. I went back into the hiding place and tried to keep the children from looking out and seeing the smoke. I promised them that someone would come see about us, but I didn't know if that would happen or not.

Well, we stayed where we were for what seemed like a long time. I sang a little Sunday school song for the children and they tried to teach me a song that their mothers sing to them to get them to fall asleep. I had heard Wali and Quatie sing it enough that I really did know it, but I pretended not to so they could "teach" me. That's what we were doing and the children were laughing at the mistakes I made (on purpose) – I told you that they could laugh and make noise with me – when I heard the sound of one horse walking (and snorting) and it was coming toward us!

The children all got quiet and I peeked out from our hiding place and saw Dog Shoot looking for us. He was calling my name, but so low that I could hardly hear him. When I saw him, I told the children to stay put (in Cherokee talk, which surprised them) and I ran out to where Dog Shoot was. He got off his horse and I ran up to him and hugged him real hard!

He seemed as glad to see me as I was to see him, but he was acting kinda strange. I didn't know what that meant, but I found out soon enough! We gathered the children and walked back toward the cabins. I wondered what had burned but I knew it wouldn't do any good to ask – Dog

Shoot wouldn't answer me, and I'd find out soon enough anyway.

When we got closer to the cabins I heard the strangest noise I've ever heard. I could tell it was women's voices but they weren't saying words. It was just a noise. It was high and long and sounded more like they were saying "oh" but all long like "oooooh." I don't know how to describe it but it was sad and scary both at the same time. I looked at Dog Shoot and so did the little kids, but he just shook his head and looked real sad.

In just a minute we would see that Mr. Bench's cabin was the one that had burned. There was nothing left but the tall stone chimney. Nothing else was burned. And then I saw Sookie and Wali, and Quatie. They were making that terrible noise! They were sitting on the ground around something covered by a blanket from one of the other cabins.

Without even looking, I knew it must be Mr. Bench and that he must be dead. I walked up to where they were and sat down by Sookie and put my arms around her. Now I knew that what they were doing must be wailing. I read in the Bible that at the end of time there will be weeping, and wailing, and gnashing of teeth. I did plenty of weeping and the women did the wailing. I don't know what gnashing of teeth means but it was the end of time for Mr. Bench.

I really don't know if I loved Mr. Bench or not, but he was good to me. He took me into his own home and gave me Christmas presents. I think he really liked me. I know my momma would fuss at me and say, "This isn't about you," but all I can say is how I felt about Mr. Bench dying – and it was just awful.

That's why I say that I will never wish for excitement again! I do wish we could all go back – even one day - to when things were the way they used to be. But I know we can't. All I can do is pray that Jesus will take care of dear, sweet Mr. Bench and that He'll find room for him in Heaven.

We are Presbyterians and back in Alabama our preacher taught us that it's not how good we are that gets us into heaven, but how good Jesus is. I sure hope that's true!

Entry 18

Now it's been a few days since Mr. Bench was killed and the cabin was burned and we have been really busy.

That same day the men buried Mr. Bench on a little rise of ground east of where the cabins were. That night the women and children stayed in one of the little cabins and the men and big boys kept watch – all night I guess – in case the bad men came back. They didn't, and the next day we packed up everything and left.

When I say everything, I mean it! The Indians didn't have big wagons like were on the trip from Alabama, but they did have one smaller flat wagon that Mr. Bench took when he went to sell the salt and to bring back supplies.

Anyway, we loaded up all the food from the smokehouse and from the cave beside the big creek and especially every bit of salt we had ready, which was a lot because it had rained so much all winter long. We wrapped everything in every scrap we could find and herded the cows and goats and all the animals together. I didn't know it before, but all the dogs at the cabins do more than hunt – they herded the other animals. I don't know if they did it naturally or if the men had trained them, but they were good at it.

Once we had everything packed – all I had left was my satchel with the Bible, my journals, pencils, papers and Anna in it – we left the little cabin area. The last thing the men did was to set the three little cabins on fire. I don't know why they did that, but once they burned there won't be anything left to show that we were ever there – even Mr. Bench's grave will soon be grown over and no one else will know where it is.

I don't really know why we left the cabin place like we did. I thought and thought about it and thought of a couple of things, but they might both be wrong. Maybe we didn't want anyone else to know where the salt was – or, and this is the scary one – they may come back looking for us. No, that wouldn't be the reason to wipe everything out. They knew where we had been and when we left, we had to take the road so anybody would know which way we went.

I know that what I'm writing doesn't make any difference – I guess I just don't want to tell what happened next. Not because it was so bad, not compared to Mr. Bench's death, but because I'm a little ashamed of how I acted.

Entry 19

We started down the road – or trace – and it was the same trace that was north of my old cabin. I kept getting more and more nervous, but Sookie and the others were so sad that I tried to be quiet. When we passed by the grape vines where Dog Shoot picked me up, I couldn't keep from starting to cry. When I did, Dog Shoot, who was riding his horse (and I was walking) came back to where I was and got down off his horse.

He asked me what was wrong (we were talking ½ English and ½ Cherokee). I tried to get him to understand that I wanted to go where my parents and the rest of my family lived.

He just kept saying, "They're all gone. No one there." I said I just wanted to see the cabins. Again he said, "No." He said they were like Mr. Bench's. I think he meant they were burned. So I just cried and cried. I couldn't help it, but Dog Shoot is not as wise or as nice as Mr. Bench was and he just didn't understand. By this time everyone else had gone on down the road and just Dog Shoot and I were there by the grape vines. He just was not going to let me see the place where I used to live.

I did a really childish thing. I took off my bonnet and threw it down on the ground in the dirt of the road. I just stared at Dog Shoot. He reached down and picked it up. Then he looked at me and held the bonnet out to me. We just stared at each other for the longest time. I'm real stubborn, but Dog Shoot may be even more stubborn!

After just a minute he said, "Mr. Bench say," and pushed the bonnet toward me. I guess he's not as dumb as I thought. No one else but me ever called him "Mr." Bench and Dog Shoot must have known that saying that would make me mind him. Anyway, I put the bonnet back on and tucked my hair up in it. Then we started walking after the others. I kept turning around and looking toward where I used to live, but I couldn't see anything. If it takes me the rest of my life, I promise I will come back here some day and find the place where my real family (instead of my Indian family) lived.

Entry 20

It took us four days to get where we were going. We had to go real slow because of the little kids. Their mothers carried them some of the way, but they had to walk by themselves part of the time. We followed the trace all the way to Duwali's village. When we got there, I found out that all villages are alike. Real towns, like we had back in Alabama and in Nacogdoches have stores in the middle and other buildings.

There the houses where people live are built sort of around the town part. In our little family village or in Mr. Bench's village and now in Duwali's, the center of the village was the main man's house – my grandfather's, Mr. Bench's, and Duwali's. All around were other, smaller cabins. I guess it would be different if there were stores, but there weren't.

When we finally reached Duwali's village, we didn't see him at first. Our little group was met with joy, tears – all the things you would expect at a family reunion. I remember back home in Alabama when there was a funeral. All the relatives would come for the funeral and my granny Williams would always talk about how the whole family seemed to get together for funerals instead of something happy. It seems like we should not be so happy at such a sad time.

Well, it felt the same way when we got to Duwali's. Everyone was very sad about Mr. Bench's death, but at the same time, they were so glad to see each other. I'll tell you later the strange thing I learned about Indian (at least Cherokee) families.

Right now it seems the sadness will never end! At least we still have Duwali! We didn't see him for several days after we arrived (at least I didn't). I don't know why, but he finally sent for me one evening. I lost my calendar in the fire, so I am not sure just what day it was. He hugged me (something most Cherokee Indians don't do) and he let me sit on his lap. We talked a little while and he promised me a new calendar and to keep on giving me plenty of paper.

He said he wanted me to keep on teaching his people, but that this was a bad time right now. I asked if what he was talking about was Mr. Bench being dead. For some reason, Cherokees don't ever say "dead." Then Duwali said something that nearly killed me! He said something like, "Yes, Bench is gone!"

Well, that's what everyone has been saying about my family all the time I have been with the Indians: that they are gone, all gone. I guess I've been stupid, but I thought my family had gone away or been kidnapped or that they thought I was dead or lost of something. Now that I know they are dead, the hurting for them is starting all over again!

I asked Duwali if my family was gone the way Bench was gone. He didn't answer with a "yes" or a "no," but he put his arms around me and let me cry some more. He finally said for me to go to bed – that he had to meet with some important men and that we would talk tomorrow night.

I didn't sleep much, if at all, that night. I just kept thinking about my family and never seeing any of them again. That makes it especially important that I keep on writing in my journal. No matter how long it takes, I solemnly promise to go back to Alabama and bring my journals to you, Granny, so you can know what happened to our family and so that you will know that I am still alive and that I love you.

The next day finally passed; it got dark (the days are getting longer) and I was sent for by Duwali. When I saw him, I told him that I had some questions. He assured me that he would answer if he knew the answer. My first question was, "Who killed my family?" He admitted that he did not know for sure, but because he is the chief of all the Cherokee Indians in this area, he knew they were not Cherokees. He said reports he had received said that there were some white men, some Mexicans, and some other (not Cherokee) Indians. When I asked "why," he said he did not know. Then he got a little less talkative. I asked if the same group had killed Mr. Bench, and he said he didn't know. I kept on asking and he finally said, "Maybe."

Then I wanted to know why they came after Mr. Bench. He gave me several answers, but he wouldn't look me straight in the eye. He said maybe they wanted the salt that Mr. Bench made, or maybe they wanted to settle down where he lived because of the good farming land or the good hunting and fishing. It just didn't sound exactly right to me so I asked him if maybe they were coming to kill me, since I was the only Killough family member left. He would just say that he did not know what they were thinking of or what they wanted any more than he knew who they were. He promised that he would keep me safe.

Then it was time for me to leave and he handed me my bonnet, even though it was dark. It finally dawned on me that maybe I had to cover my blond hair in order to help protect me against the bad men. I'll never forget my bonnet or refuse to wear it again because I may be the reason Mr. Bench died and I don't want to put Duwali or Dog Shoot or any of the other Cherokees in danger.

A strange time passed. Duwali and his helpers were gone for days at a time and then some white men came to the village to talk with Duwali. I don't know what it was about, but the men were very serious and I stayed out of sight and wore my bonnet all the time. I think the Cherokee are in big trouble with the Texas government. I don't understand what is wrong or how it will work out.

Entry 21

I promised to tell you something strange about the Cherokee, and I will, but I didn't understand it at all. The Cherokee families are not anything like ours. There is a big chief (like Duwali) that everyone minds. He tells them where to live (they move around a lot) and what to do. It's kinda like Grandpa Killough and the men of the family deciding to leave Alabama and go to Texas. But then it is all different.

If the mother Cherokee and the daddy Cherokee have children, the mother raises the girls and the uncles (the mother's brothers) raise the boys, not the boys' daddies. When we got here to Duwali's, Mr. Bench's wives went to live with their families. I guess that was o.k., but Mr. Bench had some relatives of his own, but they had nothing to do with Sookie or Wali or Quatie.

Now I don't know whether to talk to Duwali – he's very, very busy and is gone a lot – and tell him that I will testify that the Cherokees have been kind to me and have protected me against the real bad men and that one of the Cherokees even died because he was protecting me. I'm just a kid and I don't know if anybody would even listen to me. Also, I don't have anybody to talk to – Mr. Bench is dead, Duwali is too busy, and I've never thought Dog Shoot is too awfully smart. I guess I'll find Sookie and see what she says.

Well, I've talked to Sookie and I'm not completely happy with what she had to say, but I am more impressed with how much she seems to know and understand. After I explained everything I know to her, she told me that I didn't know the most important fact! She said that the

Texas government wants all the land the Cherokees live on. She thinks that the government really knows that the Cherokees didn't have anything to do with the death of my family, but they are pretending to think that so that they will have an excuse to chase the Cherokees out of Texas. Sookie says that there is a place across a big river called the Indian Territory and if the Texas government drives us out of Texas, that's where we will have to go. But then she looked at me kind of funny and said, "Of course, you're white."

That gives me a whole new problem to think about. If I had a choice, would I choose to be white or Cherokee? I just have too much on my mind. I guess I miss my momma most of all my first family. She would tell me what to do, and it would be the right thing – but I don't have her. Sookie said something that reminded me so much of Momma. She said, "Be a child; let the grownups worry about grownup problems. They are too big for you."
So, for as long as I can, I'm just going to be a little girl.

We have moved, permanently I guess, into Duwali's village. I still miss Mr. Bench and my life at his village, but this is pretty nice. Right now I don't have any teaching to do. I have made some friends and still have some of my old ones. Sookie is still my best older friend and I like her little girl, but I never see Chooch since he is now spending all his time with one of his uncles (Sookie's brother) who is teaching him all about hunting and stuff like that. I thought he already knew all that, but I guess there's more to it than I thought.

Entry 22

The best thing about my new village is my new friends. One is Alcey. She is about a couple of years older than I am – I still have trouble with the Cherokee Indians' idea of time, or really the fact that they don't care about time.

You're either a kid or you're old enough to get married, or you are a grownup, or you are old and your family takes care of you. That's all that matters to them. It's so different from what I am used to. I was born on September 2, 1828, and it is now it is late spring of 1839, so I'll soon be 11 years old. My new friend Alcey acts like she's a little bit older, I'd guess about 12. We have lots of fun playing like grownup women.

Then I have another new friend, too. Her name is Ancih, and I think she's probably 10 years old. So, I have two new girl friends, one older than me, and one younger. Ancih and I still play with dolls – and I like that a lot. Alcey has taught me something new that I really like. I already knew how to make salt, but there aren't any boggy places here, so I don't ever get to do that any more and I kinda already knew how to make pots a little bit, but Alcey is really good at making dishes. We go down to a pretty big creek and dig up some clay. Then we add enough water to it to keep it moist enough to work with our hands and we shape it into pots and bowls and cups and plates. Since we started, I've gotten good and Alcey has really gotten even better than she was to start with. We make stripes and other designs on the dishes. Then we set them out to dry, covered with damp leaves. Once they dry all the way through, they are hard and they really look good. Now I'm teaching Alcey how to knit.

Sookie had already taught me to sew, so I make clothes for myself and my friends when I'm with Alcey. When I'm playing with Ancih, we make pretty clothes for our dolls. Mine is "store-bought", but Ancih's is home made. Her mother and her big sister made it and it's really pretty but Anna is still my favorite.

Most days at Duwali's the grownups act like they want us to go play and stay out of the way. The men and boys spend all their time practicing their hunting and shooting. That kinda worries me, but the most worrisome thing is that strangers (always white men) are always coming to see Duwali when he's here. A lot of time he's gone – I guess he's meeting with white men off somewhere else. When I think about it, it's scary. There's a lot of arguing among the Indian men. They even argue with Duwali.

Entry 23

Things just get more and more scary. Ancih told me that her big sister said it looks like there will be a war between the Indians and the white men. The only war I ever heard anything about was America's war with England for our freedom. When Elizabeth was our teacher on the wagon train from Alabama -- Talledega, Alabama – I wrote that because I had not thought about Talledega in a long time and I don't ever want to forget about it.

Anyway, Elizabeth taught us all about the American Revolution because the boys liked to hear about it and would listen to Elizabeth during that part of the lessons. I don't know what's going to happen. Will the white men dress up in uniforms like the Red Coats did? Will the Cherokees shoot from behind trees like the Americans did? Surely the Americans – or white men – will have learned from the American Revolution how to fight. It sounds like both sides will be fighting the same way. Maybe it will make a difference who has the most men.

Well, everywhere I've been in Texas except Nacogdoches, there's mostly been Indians, so it looks from my own experience like there are more Indians than white people in Texas. I don't know if there are other big towns in Texas like Nacogdoches with just white people in them or not. Everybody has always told me that I worry too much, but I can't help it.

I also wonder where a battle, or war, or fight takes place. Do the women and children stay at the village while the men go to some place to fight? Or do the women and children go hide while the men fight at the village? From what I know about battles, the winner burns the cabins.

At least in the case of my family, they killed everybody and burned the cabins. I only escaped because I wasn't there. Then, when Mr. Bench was killed, the bad men only killed him and burned his cabin. The only thing I know for sure is that if there is a war, I'm going to keep Anna and my satchel safe. My satchel has gotten fat, but I'll clean it out today so that all I will have in it is my Bible, my journals, and my pencils and paper. Right now it has a lot of school papers in it from when I was teaching at Mr. Bench's.

Entry 24

I do know one good thing though and that is that Dog Shoot and Wali have gotten married! I didn't go to the wedding – I don't know what an Indian wedding is like, but they moved into a cabin together. So I guess they had a wedding. I went to some weddings in Alabama and they were beautiful!

If Dog Shoot had asked me, I could have told him what a really nice wedding is like – with flowers and pretty dresses and punch and cake afterwards. Then the big boys have a shiveree, but I don't really know much about that except that they (the big boys) make a lot of noise and try to scare the couple.

I don't think I've ever seen an Indian scared. I've seen them sad – like when Mr. Bench died, and angry – like I sometimes make Dog Shoot, and I've seen them being gentle to their babies and being kind to me but I've never seen a grown Indian scared. But from my experience the day that Mr. Bench got killed, and I had to keep the children safe, maybe grownups do get scared, but they just don't let the young ones know it.

Anyway, big things are happening. The first corn is ripe and all the women and children are harvesting it. It is very, very hot. I don't have a calendar, but from the heat, the length of the days, and the corn being ripe, it must be about the middle of the summer.

We are all packing up for a big move, but if anybody knows where were going, they aren't telling me I asked Wali and she said she really doesn't know. Dog Shoot just told her to pack everything up. I told you before that Indians don't talk much, and this is one of those times that it really bothers me.

Anyway, I have cleaned out my satchel like I said I would and have been reading my Bible a lot. I guess God really loves me because there were many times that I could have gotten killed and I wasn't, so I guess if I read His book, several things will happen: it really comforts me (doesn't that sound just like you talking, Granny?), it helps me brush up on my English, and just maybe I'll understand what is happening a little better. There are lots of stories in the Bible that remind me of the Cherokees and of my life here.

We are all moving at last. It took a week or so to pack up and gather all the ripe corn and such, but now we're all moving north, sorta back toward Mr. Bench's village, or where it was. All I hear is "war," so I guess you go some place to fight a war. What I don't really understand is why the whole village (and it's a pretty big one) is going. It would make more sense to me if the men just went to the war and maybe left just a few of them to guard us and then all came back after the fighting was over.

The other thing I keep hearing (this is where you would say, "little pitchers have big ears) is the name "Indian Territory." I don't know where it is. I know what territory means, so I guess it means that's where the Indians live, or that's land that they own, or something like that.

Entry 25

One thing I've learned from the Indians is patience. I still think all the time, but I'm being quieter about it – like an Indian. Maybe they think all the time, too. I never thought of that. I just thought they didn't know anything to say.

So we are still going north. I think we are past where my family was killed and Mr. Bench was killed – for two reasons. First, we've been traveling for six days and really traveling pretty fast and it only took us four days to get from Mr. Bench's to Duwali's. But the real reason is that at one time Dog Shoot rode back to where I was walking with Wali and Quatie and got down off his horse and walked with us. I got the idea that he was watching me. That made me think we were near where my family lived. Then, after a long time, he got back on his horse (it's a pretty brown and white pinto) and rode close to us for a while. The next day he rode like he always does.

The women and children walk in he middle with the wagons and animals and the men ride their horses along the outside edges. I guess this is to protect us, but I really don't know. I wish I were riding a horse, or even in a wagon. It's so hot and dusty, but only the old people and the babies and very little children ride on the wagons.

We have finally gotten to our destination. At least, we have stayed two nights in the same place and we have set up camp. No one is attempting to cut trees and build cabins, so I guess we are not going to settle here, but we're all tired and hot and dusty so we're glad to stop for a little while. Just like when we left Mr. Bench's village, we have brought all the meat from the smokehouses and all the potatoes and things from the root cellars, so I guess we aren't going back to where Duwali had his village.

Entry 26

Granny, in some ways all sorts of different people are really alike in some ways. Do you remember back in Talledega that everyone had a root cellar out in the yard that they stored things like potatoes, onions, rutabagas, and stuff in?

Then if there was a bad storm, everyone would go down in the root cellar to hide? Well, the Cherokee Indians have root cellars just like that, and there was one at Duwali's village. But the funny thing is that every so often, Grandpa Williams or Grandpa Killough would make the big boys go down there to clear out the varmints that were living there. Well, the Cherokees do the same thing and the big Indian boys act just like the boys back in Alabama did.

They bring out snakes and rats and spiders and throw them on the girls. The Indian girls run and scream just like we did back home. I hope the boys know which snakes and spiders are poisonous and which are not. I don't think they would really try to kill us. Duwali would be too mad!

This is a pretty nice place. There is a good creek nearby and it is spring-fed. The kids found several places where the water comes out of the ground. My daddy told me a long time ago that if the water comes up out of the ground, it is good to drink and that the creek won't go dry in the summer when it doesn't rain.

The women and some of the girls washed most of the things that were so dusty from the move. We (the younger girls) even got in the water (it was cold) to take a bath while the older women washed our clothes. I asked Sookie about my bonnet and she let me take it off to bathe and she washed it for me. When our clothes were dry, I had to put the bonnet back on.

I finally got to talk with Duwali again. On the night after our baths, there was a big campfire and meeting of all the men after we ate. I guess Sookie knows how curious I am (I have hidden and listened to the men talk more than once), so she gave me plenty to do to keep me away from the meeting.

When we were through cleaning up from supper, Dog Shoot came and got me and took me to Duwali. All the men from the camp were still there and Duwali took me on his lap to sit. He and I talked (in English) for a while and here's what he told me: "There is going to be a big battle tomorrow near where we are now." He said all the men had voted to fight. I asked if that was what he wanted to do and he said it didn't matter what he wanted – that he was just one voice (I think he meant one vote).

Anyway, he said the battle will be between the Indians and the Texian Army (the white men). So he said I had a very serious decision to make. He said if I wanted to go live with the white people, all I had to do was let them see me and my hair. If I wanted to stay with the Cherokee, I had to hide who I was. He said the Cherokee need me to teach them English. He said he was proud to have me as his granddaughter. Then we were quiet for a while. When we finally started talking again, I told him that I had been thinking, reading my Bible, and praying every night for the right decision. I told him that I read two things in my Bible that told me what I should decide.

In the New Testament I read what Jesus said about "I was hungry and you fed me; I was homeless and you took me in," and so on. I also told Duwali that one of my favorite stories from the Old Testament is about Ruth and Naomi. The prettiest words – maybe in the whole Bible are: "Whither thou goest, I will go; whither thou lodgest, I will lodge; thy people shall be my people and thy God, my God."

Of course, I plan to try to make my God their God, but the rest of it is true for me. I think the Cherokees saved my life at least twice. They took me in, gave me a home, and gave me a new family. I want to live with the Cherokees. Even though I am still very young, this is my decision forever. Duwali hugged me hard and then he told the Indian men sitting around that I was to be given every courtesy, and was to be considered his own flesh and blood. He told them that he was a very old man and that he didn't think he would come back from the battle alive – that's when I started crying.

Entry 27

After he finished talking to the men, he called Dog Shoot over and told him that he would not take part in the battle the next day, but that his job was to stay at the camp to protect the women and children. Dog Shoot started to argue, but Duwali held up his hand to make Dog Shoot be quiet. Duwali said Dog Shoot was to be the boss over the salt – that is the most important thing we own, and that his special job was to watch over me. Then when Dog Shoot opened his mouth to argue some more, Duwali said, in a very loud voice: "Duwali say." Dog Shoot looked at me and I kinda smiled because that's what he said to me one time to make me mind. He saw the smile on my face and just nodded his head.

Duwali and all the men and big boys left the next day. I don't know exactly where they are going to have their fight, but they rode west. The women, children and their guards (there were more than just Dog Shoot, but he was in charge of the guards) stayed behind.

A couple of worrisome, very slow, days passed. Then the next day a very few Cherokees returned to camp. Duwali was not with them but Chooch was. The rest of that day was confused and confusing. That night the men had a big campfire and a pow-wow. Then the next day the Texian soldiers arrived at the camp.

Because I can speak both languages, I hid and listened (with Dog Shoot's o.k.). Later we discussed what I heard the Texians say.

The Texians told the Indians – through an interpreter – that they were there to escort the Cherokees to the Indian

Territory, and that they could never come back to Texas. When the Indians asked about their land, houses, etc., the head Texian said, "To the victor go the spoils." Dog Shoot and I discussed this and Dog Shoot said that the Cherokees had lost the war and the Texians had won, and what they had won was everything that the Indians had.

I asked what had happened in the battle, but Dog Shoot said he had not heard the whole story yet, but he did know that nearly all the Cherokee were killed (he said "gone" of course.)

We packed up again and headed north, escorted by the army men. It is a sad time, but a familiar one. We travel just like we had done when we left Bench's village and Duwali's with one difference.

We didn't travel so fast. Without any planning, the Indians all slowed down. When the soldiers tried to hurry the Indians, they just went slower. The soldiers did not seem to know what to do. I guess they were told not to hurt the Indians.

Entry 28

I am very careful not to let the army men see me closely enough to see that I am white. I always walk in a group instead of by myself. I even sleep in my bonnet, and I got Dog Shoot and Wali to cut my hair pretty short. I had watched Dog Shoot sharpening his knife and he had it so sharp that it didn't even pull when he cut my hair.

The army had taken away all the men's guns. They did something to them and then gave them back to the Indians. Dog Shoot showed me that the rifles would not shoot because of something on the trigger. He said when we get to Indian Territory, they will take the "locks" off and then they could hunt again. He said if the army men caught an Indian with the lock off his gun before we get to the Indian Territory, the army man would kill the Indian right away.

I know it sounds like Dog Shoot talked a lot, but it took a lot of asking and a lot of time to get all this out of him. The thing with the rifles makes me explain something else to you. You remember that we took all the corn, the smokehouse and root cellar food with us from Duwali's. But the Indians pretended that they did not have any food and couldn't hunt without their rifles, so the army had to supply food for the whole village.

There must have been about 100 people in the march to Indian Territory by now. We kept getting more Indians and more army men along the way. It got to be so many people that it was confusing to us – or at least to me – and was getting harder and harder for the army men to get enough food to feed us. When you have that many people moving along, they pretty much scare all the wild animals away.

When we came upon a settler, the army took everything they could – cows, pigs, food from the smokehouse, and anything else they wanted. I don't know if they paid the settlers or not, but I guess not.

It finally got so bogged down that the army split the Indians up into groups of about 30. This only happened after several campfires and meetings with the Indians. Of course, the Indians knew how to split themselves up and the army did not.

We were camped for the second day at a pretty good place – I'll tell you later what the land is like. One group of Indians and their army men moved to the north. Dog Shoot came to me and asked if I knew what a week is. I said, "Sure. It's seven days – or seven sleeps." He nodded and I asked why he wanted to know and he told me that was how the Indian groups would be leaving, one every week. I asked if we could be the next group to leave. He asked me why and I said, the last group to go won't find any wild animals for the army to kill for us to eat, and even the settlers wouldn't have any food left for us. He said he would see.

Entry 29

I guess he persuaded the interpreters that he could have his group ready to go next because he had us start packing to move the next morning. He and the other grownup Cherokees from Duwali's village – even the women – had a big campfire last night. Of course, I hid and listened.

Dog Shoot told them (in the Indian language) that he was taking the salt and the food and would be leaving soon. He invited those who wanted to come with him. But he said if you go with your clan (he was talking to the women now), the salt and food do not go with you.

After it was all over, the ones going with us were Dog Shoot, me, Wali, Wakie, and Quakie and Quatsie and her clan, plus a couple of grownup Indian men. It made me sad, but Sookie and Sally were going with Sookie's clan -- I guess because she wanted to see Chooch, who was being raised by one of Sookie's brothers.

Good news at last! We packed up some more today and tonight the army men came to talk to Dog Shoot. They said his group was too small, so the army men were going to put our little group together with another group about the same size. Afterward Wali told me that she thinks it will be Sookie's clan. There are 20 of us and 9 of them. That means we will still have Sookie and Chooch and Sally with us.

I didn't write yesterday because we were busy and it was after dark before we went to bed. Today we moved out. There are about 30 people in our group. We have all our provisions (hidden from the army men, of course) and my best friends. It turns out that Alcey and Ancih are both in Sookie's clan, so they are going with us! This gives me someone to play with. It turns out that they are first cousins to each other, but they don't know what that means.

I promised to tell you about the land we are traveling through. We always go north. The land is getting flatter and poorer. It isn't red dirt any more but kinda gray – at least where it is dry. When it's wet, it's kinda black, but not rich looking. I don't think it will grow much. It's still hot summer, but I don't see very many crops, and we aren't following in the tracks of the first group that left. They headed a little to the northwest and we are going pretty much due north with a tiny bit to the east.

The soldiers don't associate with the Indians. At night they give us whatever they have been able to find for us to eat, and then move a little ways off. The Indians build a fire, cook their food, eat, and then sit around the campfire. The army men do the same thing, but far enough away that they can see us, but not hear us. We can't hear them either.

Tonight Chooch told the story of the battle. Then we all went to bed.

Entry 30

Today we broke camp and continued to move north. I'm tired of the slow pace, so I found Sookie and we talked about the move. Sookie said that we wanted to save all the food, salt, and supplies that we could for the Indian Territory because we didn't know what it would be like.

I asked her why we were going so slow and she tried to explain that we know Texas and like it – I know I really don't want to leave it – so we take as long as we can. She repeated something I had already heard – once we leave Texas we (at least the Indians) can never come back. I don't feel exactly the same. I know and understand the grownups' feelings, but the kids are all ready for a new adventure.

Tonight was just like last night. After we ate, Chooch told the story of the battle again. After the campfire broke up, I sat by myself and thought a while. Everyone is so used to my writing in my journal that they pretty much leave me alone after we eat.

Anyway, I finally figured out that the Indians can't write, so they have to learn the stories they want to keep and that by Chooch repeating the story over and over, the people listening will learn it and can tell it to others, especially their children so that the story – the history of their people -- won't be lost.

Well, I can write, so I will. Here is what Chooch told us about the battle.

The first day of the battle there were more Indians than Texians, but the Texians had better guns, more bullets, and were fierce fighters. The Indians were driven off and retreated to a place near a Kickapoo Indian settlement. The second day the Texians caught up with the Indians and there was a short, fierce battle. Duwali rode his sorrel horse with the blaze face and four white feet, up and down the lines, urging his men to battle. He wore a Mexican officer's hat, a sword, a sash, and a silk vest that a man named Sam Houston had given him. When the lines of Indians broke, he tried to get them to fight again. Duwali's horse was shot from under him and he was shot in the thigh. As he limped from the field of battle, he was shot in the back. He sat down and leaned back against the trunk of a tree, facing the enemy. Then one of the Texians shot him in the head, killing him instantly.

When he fell dead, the rest of the Indians lost their will to fight and fled the field of battle.

And that's the story of the last battle of the war. I don't know what it will be called in history, but I'm both proud and sad. Of course I'm sad because Duwali is dead and I'm amazed that such an old man was so tough and hard to kill. I'll always be proud of him and his actions and proud that he was my grandfather.

Entry 31

We continued north with the same routine. The army keeps on finding food for us, but it isn't very much or very good. When the women cook the food, they try to save back a little that will keep without spoiling to eat when we are in the Indian Territory.

I want to tell you this, Granny, about a talk I had with Sookie. We were walking along this morning in the middle of the women when I asked her why some women didn't like me. She said it was true that some of them did not like me much, but they were the ones who didn't know me. She told me that some of the people I meet won't like me and it has nothing to do with me – I won't have done anything wrong. She said the problem is with them, not me. I'm really not sure what she means, but it sounded real wise. She kept on talking and explained that every time the Cherokees go somewhere that there are white people, they face the same thing. Eventually they have to leave and to leave everything they have worked for.

Today was the last day we spent in Texas. We arrived at the river that divides Texas from the Indian Territory. I don't know the name, but it is much, much smaller than the Mississippi.

After we got there, there was a lot of milling around. First, everyone and the wagons had to get lined up. Then Dog Shoot had to talk to the army men and the army men showed the Indian men how to take the "locks" off their guns I guess the Texian men were okay after all because they gave the Indians all the bullets they could spare. Then it was time to cross the river. As I said, it is not as deep or as wide as the Mississippi and it is late summer and it has been dry. Anyway, I hung back while the others crossed. I sat on a little hillock with my journal, pretending to write because I knew everyone would leave me alone if they thought I was writing. But I wasn't really writing – what I was really doing was crying. I didn't act like a big girl and I'm ashamed of that, but all I could think of was all I have lost –my family, Mr. Bench, Duwali – all of them in Texas, and I've even lost Texas now!

Entry 32

Finally, everyone and everything else was across the river and they were looking for a good place to make camp. It was late afternoon and I'm sure everyone was as tired as I was. Then Dog Shoot rode up to where I was sitting, got down off his horse, and sat down beside me, looking across the river into the Indian Territory. Being Dog Shoot, and Cherokee, he didn't say anything for a long time. Finally he said, "Are you sure?"

I had to think about that a little while and then when I decided that he meant did I want to cross the river and live with the Indians or stay on this side and be all white, I said, "I'm sure." We were both quiet for a little longer and Dog Shoot said, "We'd better go."

I told him there was something else he didn't know about. I now think of myself as ½ Indian. And I want to go with the Cherokees and live with them, but I'm scared.

In a way I'm eager to leave Texas. I know Texas meant a new home and a new beginning and even a better life for Daddy and Granddaddy and my uncles, but all it means to me is death and loss. Everyone I've ever loved, except for you, Granny, died in Texas. If I stay here in this country, I would be afraid of loving anyone. With my luck, they would get killed, too.

All the things that Texas meant to my family are the things I hope for in Indian Territory. All the little kids think going to the Indian Territory will be exciting, and I have enough kid in me to be a little bit excited about that.

Anyway, I told Dog Shoot that I am scared of crossing the river. When Dog Shoot looked at me funny, I told him about crossing the Mississippi. I haven't even told you about this, and I haven't thought about it in a long, long time. I had nearly forgotten, but now I remember and here's what happened.

When we crossed the Mississippi River, I told you how we went real far north, the men built a raft, loaded a wagon and horses on it, and floated it down and a little to the west so that they got across the river near where they wanted to. The women and children would cross on a different raft. The reason for that, according to Daddy, was that the raft with the wagon was more dangerous than the people raft. I know that is true because of something that happened and I saw it.

We were far north on the east side of the river and the kids were watching the men and big boys build the heavy rafts and load them with the horses and wagons. They loaded this one wagon and the man and his oldest son rode on the raft holding the lead horses' heads so they wouldn't get scared. Well, the current was strong, the river was wide, and the man and his boy weren't able to keep the horses still. The lead horses tried to get loose and they spooked the two horses behind them and the commotion of the four horses trying to bolt made the raft swing around and it was broadside to the current when it turned over.

Household goods were thrown out and floated downstream. I never saw the man and boy after that. The horses were hitched together and to the heavy wagon and it pulled them down and drowned them.

Daddy and the other men rode a long way down the river, but most of the stuff that fell into the water was broken or ruined. They sent us kids to our mamas while Daddy, Granddaddy, and some others went to the woman whose husband and son had died. They didn't come back until the next morning and we never saw the widow and the rest of the family again. I don't know where they went or who took care of them. When any of us asked Daddy about it, he would get mad. Mother said he wasn't mad at us, but was upset because it could have been one of our family that that happened to. She forbade us to ever mention it again and I guess I had forgotten about it until now.

After I told Dog Shoot why I was afraid to cross the river, he put me up on his horse, got on behind me and turned my head so I couldn't see ahead. I put my arms around his neck and shut my eyes. We rode across the river at a shallow place.

And so we left Texas behind.

Part Two
Indian Territory

Entry 33

After we got across the river, we continued until the land rose sharply. The Texian Army men stayed on the Texas side of the river and watched us as we crossed the river and climbed the bank. When we were high enough above the river that the bugs would not bite us, we made camp and started a fire with the embers we have been keeping alive since we left Duwali's village. The Army men spent the night across the river and left the next morning.

As it turned out, this spot would be our camp for the next several days. We didn't know where we were or where we were supposed to go or if we should stay here. While the women and children rested and took care of chores, Dog Shoot and some of the men, including Chooch, went to check out the area and find out what they could. Dog Shoot took some salt with him in his blanket roll to use for bargaining and trading.

While the men were gone, Alcey, Ancih, and I had time to play with our dolls and to sew some clothes for the dolls and for us. Alcey is a year or two older than I am, but she acts like an old grandmother. We tried on clothes and she had some that no longer fit her, but they would fit me. Some of my clothes now will fit Ancih, so I gave them to her. That left us with only Alcey to make clothes for. It was fun making patterns, cutting them out and sewing them.

As much as Alcey is like a grandmother and is very serious, Ancih is young for her age. She laughs and talks all the time. Sometimes she is talking Cherokee – and when that happens, Alcey scolds her and tells her to practice speaking English. Most of the time Ancih just giggles and switches over to English – for a while. She talks so fast that when she comes to a word that she can't remember in English, she will say it in Cherokee and then keep on talking in Cherokee. Alcey and I both baby her and never get too mad at her. How can you be mad at someone who is always laughing and hugging you?

We talked about what lay ahead for us. Of course, we had no idea, so we would make up wild dreams. A handsome man would come along and would be enchanted by our beauty and grace and would take us away to be his wife. He would always be rich and we would never have to work again. He would have so many slaves that we wouldn't have to lift a finger all day. We would have perfect children who never cried or gave us any trouble (of course, the house slaves would take care of them when we were visiting or sewing or doing something like that.)

I tried to tell Alcey and Ancih about parties that I had seen back in Alabama, but that was so long ago that I didn't do a very good job. My sister Elizabeth and my older cousins would have parties, and picnics, and things like that when the work on the farms was done, but I only got to watch from a hiding place. No really young children were allowed. By the time we moved to Texas, I was only about 9 years old – still too young to go to the parties.

One night after my two friends had to go to their own families, I started thinking about my birthday. Surely it must be soon. Then I'll be eleven. Since Alcey and Ancih don't know how old they are, when I turn eleven, I'll just think of them as being 12 and 10. I tried once to explain birthdays to them. I guess I didn't do too good a job. They didn't understand at all.

Entry 34

After being gone four days, Dog Shoot and the men came back. It was all I could do to keep from asking what they had found out. I knew better than to act too curious. On the day they got back, after our mid-day meal, Dog Shoot came to find me and said, "We talk."

We walked a little way from our campsite and sat down on some fallen trees. We just sat for a while, and then he told me that he went to a fort and he had to speak English. The soldiers there were so glad to find an Indian who spoke English that they were nice to him and very patient in everything.

Here's what he learned: the American government had divided the Indian Territory into parts. Where we had crossed the river landed us in Choctaw territory. The Cherokees were given some land way to the north of here.

While the Choctaws and the Cherokees were pretty friendly with each other, the Choctaws probably would not like for us to settle in part of "their" land, so we would have to move north to the Cherokee territory. I don't know about the Choctaw Indians. But the Cherokees do not think that they can "own" land. To them, it is just land and they are free to come and go on it as they please. Their time in Texas got them to thinking about ownership, but they could not understand how another Indian could believe that.

After Dog Shoot and the other men left the fort – it was called Towson – they came across some Choctaw Indians, and one of them could talk a little English. Because Dog Shoot could talk to him and because he had some salt to give the man, Dog Shoot was treated pretty good. They made an arrangement so that we could cross the Choctaw land to go to the Cherokee land if we would follow a couple of rules. First, no one in our group could stay on the Choctaw land; we all had to pass through it. Second, we could kill just the number of animals we needed to eat and we had to pay – with salt – for all we killed. The man, who must have been a chief, agreed to send someone to escort us to the edge of their land and then to collect the salt to pay for the animals we killed for food.

Dog Shoot finally paid me a compliment – probably the only one I'll ever get from him. He said that it was good that he knew some English – that he never expected it to come in handy. I did not remind him that he was able to understand the soldiers that escorted us to the border of Texas and they didn't figure out he was able to know what they were saying.

Entry 35

The next day we loaded everything up in preparation to heading north. It is still hot and I haven't worn my bonnet since we crossed the river. My hair has really gotten light. I don't know what I'll do about it in the days to come. Then when our Choctaw escort showed up, Dog Shoot told me that I should cover my hair and keep out of the way of the Choctaws. My hair is such a problem.

Sookie and I talked for a little bit while we were packing everything up for the next stage of our journey. She didn't know anything that Dog Shoot told me, so I repeated it for her. Then we talked about killing animals in the Choctaw land. On one hand, we had plenty of dried meat and only a limited amount of salt. We don't know what the Cherokee land will be like. They may not have many animals for us to eat. And they may not have the right conditions for getting salt out of the ground. I'm glad I don't have to figure out what we should do, but I am happy that Dog Shoot and Sookie trust me enough to talk to me about grown-up things.

We got our guide today and started on the way to the Cherokee territory. Because of the little children, the livestock, and such, we don't go very far each day.

We have been traveling now for four days and we're not even out of Choctaw territory. The guide told Dog Shoot that we were still four or five days from the edge of the Choctaw land. We are traveling generally north, but to avoid having to go over hills, we go around. That takes us a little to the east or west, but we can see taller hills (maybe even mountains) to the east.

Today I heard good news – Dog Shoot and his wife are going to have a baby! At the slow rate we are traveling, the baby will be born before we get where we are going.

Today is the 10th day we have been traveling through Choctaw land. Finally, we are nearly at the border of it.

We have only had to kill one black bear, one deer, and one pig to eat on the way. We are trying to make our own supplies last. We might need them in Cherokee land. However, we are seeing so much in the way of streams that we should be able to find plenty of animals for food and plenty water to make salt.

Entry 36

Generally the weather has been good for our journey, but that changed today. When it would rain lightly, we would keep on going, but today we had a real storm. First we woke up to a really strong wind blowing from the West. The men kept looking at the sky and at clouds that were piling up in the West and finally decided that we would stay put for the day.

We always make camp on the side of a hill or on kinda high land – usually where we have some kind of natural protection – a hill, a ridge, a stand of trees – from the West. Now I know why. I guess I had realized that most bad weather travels from West to East, but it had not made an impression on me. Even though Elizabeth isn't here to teach me things, I can still learn --- and the Indians have plenty to teach me if I'll just pay attention.

Our camps remind me a little of my first home in Texas. Remember how I told you that Grandpa's house was in the middle with each of his children having their own cabin around his like the spokes of a wheel? Well, the Cherokee camp always has the campfire in the middle with different members of the family having their own little family area around. I live with Dog Shoot and Wali and her little girl Wakie. Sookie and Chooch are in the next place to our left – about ten (men's) paces away.

Anyway, Granny, I was going to tell you about our first big storm. The men drove the animals into a small copse of trees and with the help of the women and children, tied down or someway secured all the loose things and tried to cover everything that would ruin if it got wet.

It wasn't long before the rain began. The men went to where the animals were to try to calm them down and left the women and children to hide beneath the wagons (we have 3 now). There was some really scary lightning and lots of rain. It got much cooler and with our wet clothes, it felt very cold.

My job, as usual, was to try to keep the little children entertained. So, we started our lessons. We talked about the four points of the compass and what lay in each direction. These were my home and a really big river to the East, our recent home and Texas to the South, the storm-maker to the West, and our future home to the North. Alcey helped me, but Ancih is more like the youngsters and was not much help.

Before the rain let up, we had time for another lesson in English, although we didn't have any paper or pencils (they were packed away). After the storm passed, there was a beautiful rainbow. I told the others the story of Noah and what the rainbow means.

After the rain was over, the ground was too soggy to travel and we had some important things to do so we stayed put.

The first thing we had to do was to pay our Choctaw scout and let him go back to his home. He told us that we were officially in Cherokee territory, but I don't know how he could tell. We crossed that river from Texas into the Indian Territory, but I didn't see any kind of landmark to let us know we were in Cherokee territory.

Entry 37

I need to let you know what this territory looks like. It isn't as pretty as Texas or as Alabama. Texas looked to me like Eden, but I guess this territory is like what Adam and Eve were thrown out of Eden into.

The land is not as fertile and the trees not as big and as green. One thing this place has going for it is the water. We cross a stream or creek nearly every day. In fact, this afternoon the sun came out so Ancih and Alcey begged to go to the next creek (one Chooch had found on a short foray right after the rain stopped.) They wanted to see if they could wash the mud out of their clothes. Normally they would not have been allowed to go off by themselves, but this day, Chooch said he had seen no animals or even other Indians.

Also, usually I would have gone with them, but Sookie asked me to help her make some little baby things for Dog Shoot and Wali's baby. Sookie is good at making clothes, but I am best at needlework. Sookie had gotten hold of some soft yarn and wanted me to knit a pretty little blanket.

Here's what happened: the two friends stayed out a long time. Sookie began to get worried as the afternoon grew late. She went and found Dog Shoot, and that was strange by itself. Sookie is very quiet, like most Cherokee women, and would never have done anything to draw attention to herself. So she must have been plenty worried.

Dog Shoot, Chooch, and one other man went looking for the girls. They left the rest of the men at camp to look after the livestock and to keep an eye on the rest of the girls and women.

It was well after dark when they got back – without the girls! It may have been a hint at the seriousness of the situation that Dog Shoot called a campfire meeting for that evening. Dog Shoot explained that Chooch had led them to the creek. When they got there, there was no one around. What they did find were hoof prints made by horses and a couple of men. They also found signs that the two girls had been there.

No one said it, but I think all of us were afraid that someone had stolen the girls. The place was so muddy that our men had trouble telling how many horses had been there.

I don't think anyone got any sleep that night. Early the next morning the men, except for a couple of men armed with guns, left looking for Alcey and Ancih. At noon the searchers returned -- again empty-handed.

After we had a little to eat, they left again, but this time, Chooch and a man who searched this morning stayed to guard us and the two guards from this morning went with Dog Shoot.

We stayed camped where we were for three more days before anything happened. And they were long, worrisome days. On the fifth day since they went missing, the search party came back before nightfall with Alcey. I saw her as they rode into camp. Alcey was riding with Dog Shoot in front of him, just like I had ridden across the river from Texas. Ancih was not with them. I didn't know at that time what it meant.

Dog Shoot rode straight to Alcey's mother and let Alcey down. Alcey's family members closed in around her and

I couldn't see her anymore. Then he rode over to where Ancih's family was camped and got down and talked with Ancih's mother for a while. Then he got back on his horse and rode to our campsite. Before he got to us, I heard that high, wailing (now I know it's called "keening") that I had heard at Mr. Bench's camp. I knew what that meant without being told.

Entry 38

I cried with my doll Anna (I know I'm too old to have a doll, but it was some comfort to bury my face in her) for a little while and then I went over to Alcey's place to see her. But when I got there, the grownups would not let me. When I got back to Dog Shoot's place, it was all I could to keep from crying again. Dog Shoot came over and sat down beside me. He asked me what was wrong and I told him that they would not let me see Alcey and that I hadn't done anything wrong. So Dog Shoot tried to explain what had happened. He talked very low and in Cherokee so it took a while, but here's what he said.

Alcey and Ancih were bathing in a pool when three men rode up and caught them by surprise. They tried to run away, but were caught. I don't know exactly what all happened, but the men treated the girls like wives. (That's what Dog Shoot said in Cherokee).

Anyway, the men let the girls get their clothes and took them on the men's horses to the East. When it started to get dark, they made a camp and gave the girls some jerky to chew on.

They stayed there one night only. The next day, they moved just a little farther east and made camp again. One man left camp for a few hours and came back with a pig he had killed. Alcey and Ancih had to cook part of it for everyone's supper.

Then after supper, Ancih made a big mistake. I told you how she is such a chatterbox. Well, while she and Alcey were cleaning up after supper, Ancih was talking when she said something in English. That's the way we would talk to each other. We would be talking in one language and then if we couldn't think of a word we wanted in that language, we would switch over to the other language without thinking about it. Unfortunately, one of the men was near by and heard Ancih say something in English. He got all excited and he and the other two men beat the girls cruelly until Ancih admitted that they could speak English.

I guess you would say the cat was out of the bag (I remember you saying that when someone told a secret they shouldn't tell.) Anyway, the men wanted to know how the girls learned English. Again, it was Ancih who told them about me. They seemed quite interested in hearing about me. Of course, the three of us had talked about everything when we played or worked together. Ancih didn't know or remember every detail, but she said I was traveling with the Indians, but I wasn't an Indian – I had blond hair and green eyes and skin that was maybe a little lighter than theirs. She told them that I was special and was treated with respect even though I was only 10 years old (of all the things I had told her, that was the one she remembered). Then she said she thought I belonged to someone important.

That took a little thinking about on my part but I finally figured out that she must mean Duwali. The bad men may have thought that my real family was rich or important because Alcey heard them talking and she heard one say something about "ransom." Dog Shoot did not know that word, but I did from when we were having school on the way from Alabama to Texas.

Remember how I told you that the boys liked history because of all the battles? Well, Elizabeth told us about the knights in old England promising their king that if he got kidnapped by the enemy, they would pay his ransom to get him back.

Once I explained that to Dog Shoot, he thought about it for a while, then he made me promise that I would not wander out of sight of one of the men. It sounded to him like the bad men wanted to kidnap me and try to get ransom from somebody to let me go.

Entry 39

Anyway, to get back to Alcey and Ancih, the next day they began trying to think of a way to escape. Finally, after thinking up several plans that they knew wouldn't work, they decided to wait until after supper that night when the men were asleep and try to get away. Alcey would try to keep one of the knives hidden after she cut some meat off the pig to cook. Then she would try to cut the ropes that the men kept them tied to a tree with and they would sneak off. They would go toward the East because the men would probably look for them in the direction they came from – the West. When they thought they were safe, they would circle back and look for us.

It didn't sound like too good a plan to me, but that's what they did and it did work – up to a point. Then it all went wrong. Alcey and Ancih could not know that if they had waited just a little while Dog Shoot and the others would be there to rescue them.

Anyway, Alcey hid the knife, the men fell asleep and Alcey cut the ropes that kept them tied to a tree. The rope was stronger than she thought or the knife was duller because it took a long time to cut through it. And one of the men woke up just as the girls were sneaking away. He yelled and woke the other two. Another problem with their plan was that the moon was full and the men could see them.

There was no way the little girls could outrun the grown men, but they tried. Alcey was a little ahead of Ancih when the men began shooting! Ancih was shot at once and Alcey expected to be when she looked back and saw Dog Shoot's spotted horse and two other men with him. Dog Shoot shot one of the men, but the other two got away.

When things had settled down a little they found Ancih dead as well as the white man they had shot. Dog Shoot and his two men dug a grave and buried Ancih. They didn't bury the bad man because Dog Shoot wanted the varmints to eat his body. Then Dog Shoot set Alcey in front of him and started back to camp.

I asked Dog Shoot why Alcey -- or her family – would not let me see her. He said he wasn't sure. Maybe they blamed me for teaching the girls to talk in the bad men's language. But he really didn't know. He told me though to let the idea of seeing Alcey alone and not try to see her.

I'm not good at letting well enough alone (another one of your sayings, Granny), so I told Sookie that I needed to talk to her.

I didn't get to talk with Sookie until the next day. There was a big meeting around the main fire that night, but I wasn't allowed to go. I just felt worse and worse and cried myself to sleep with my dolly once again. I didn't even try to listen to the meeting around the campfire.

The next morning Sookie found me and we walked down to the stream. I remembered what Dog Shoot had told me, but I needn't have worried. There were adults all around and someone was always going to get water at the stream.

I asked Sookie what was wrong that Alcey's family would not let me see her and why I wasn't included in the pow wow the night before. She took her time trying to explain to me what had happened.

The Indians had had nothing but trouble since I had come along. Mr. Bench was killed (but, of course, that is not the way she said it), then Duwali, and then all the Indians were chased out of Texas – and now Ancih was killed. It seems that things just got worse and worse. Sookie said that I didn't have anyone to protect me except Dog Shoot and her.

She told me that at the pow wow the Indians decided to let me stay with them, but to not get too close to me.

Entry 40

Finally, something good happened – but it came out of something bad – a fire. As we traveled along, we came upon a burned-out building. Dog Shoot came and got me and took me though the remains of the building. At first I thought it was just a house, but once I got inside, it was a school! Of course a school would have to be near water, so the Indians made camp there.

While Sookie and the others prepared supper, Dog Shoot and I explored it. I found a dictionary, a history book, an arithmetic and a story book that were in pretty good condition. Dog Shoot said I could have whatever I wanted that wouldn't weigh us down too much.

I don't know when I've been so happy! However, since the days are getting shorter (and by the way it's getting cooler), there's not much time to read before it's too dark. I don't want to use up the newness and the excitement of them because I have no idea what lies ahead.

Something I have forgotten to tell you is how our group has grown. As we go along, we run into other groups from Texas that are going the same place we are, so we sort of travel together. I still keep to myself and try not to get out of sight of one of the men in our group.

I am being careful not to "use up" my new books, but I have learned a lot from the arithmetic book already. If I take my time, I can understand the reason behind the answers, instead of just doing the problems for the right answer. I am also making a lot of things for Wali and Dog Shoot's baby. Every time I ask Sookie for yarn, she finds me some – I don't know where it comes from, I'm just grateful for it.

We keep traveling north. We've been in Cherokee territory for a long time now and still we are not to the main Cherokee place. From reading my books, I have guessed that where we are going is the "capital" of the Cherokee territory. I don't know the name of it, or if it's a real town or a village. I think about it a lot, but until we get there I won't know if it's a town like Nacogdoches or a village, like Duwali's. Those are the two I remember most. I don't remember much about Alabama. All my memories of that time in my life except the houses of my relatives, are of the road to them, the church where we all went, and the good times I had.

I try not to think about that part of the past because it always makes me cry. But once in a while I make myself recall all I can so I won't forget. I do that at night so that no one can see me cry. I don't know what I think about that – am I torturing myself or keeping my memories?

It is getting a lot colder as we go north. I think it must not be too much father – at least I hope not.

Entry 41

Hurray! We are finally here. "Here" is a place called Tallequah. It is the capital of the Cherokee Nation. We got here yesterday evening and made camp on the edge of town. I guess I need to tell you about Tallequah –it's sort of a combination of Nacogdoches and Duwali's village.

In the center of the town are a general store, a church, a government building of some sort – kinda like a courthouse – and a school. The school is run by the church. Then, around this central part of town are the families. It's too cold to camp out. If we are going to live here, we might as well find a place and settle in. Each of the men in our group found a place to live or teamed up with someone else to build cabins.

Since Sookie and Chooch and Sally (Sookie's little girl) don't have a grown man to look out for them, Dog Shoot set out to find a place for all of us to live. He located an abandoned cabin that he thought would do us fine. It is bigger than most cabins but we have seven people – and a baby on the way. The only problem it will cause will be getting enough wood to keep it warm. Chooch told Dog Shoot that he would gather firewood and cut it if necessary as payment for letting him, his mother, and little sister live with us.

The cabin, as I told you, is quite big, even though it is only one room. The cooking is done over the fire in the fireplace. Three corners of the room are divided off with blankets or quilts. Dog Shoot and Wali and Wakie have one corner. Sookie, Chooch, and Sally have one, then mine is the smallest "room" because it is just me. That leaves a lot of room in the middle. There is a table there and four stools.

We can eat there, but not everyone has a place to sit down. I don't have a stool, nor does Wakie or Sally. It's also where we sew, have lessons and just visit.

We just sort of hung around for a couple of days to see how everything is run. Dog Shoot said "to figure out our part in the Cherokee Nation" – that's what it is called.

Entry 42

Something happened today that really upset me and the rest of our Indians. Sookie went to the general store to buy some material to sew some clothes. She asked me to come with her but to hang back and listen so I could make sure she paid the right amount. For a grown woman, she is really pretty shy. So, I pulled my bonnet over my hair and we walked from our camp place into town to the general store.

When we got into the store, I sat down on a keg of nails and Sookie went to the counter where the bolts of material were stacked. She asked – in Cherokee – how much the different materials were. The man told her the cost of each and she finally settled on a blue print. The man measured out the amount she asked for and then told her the total price.

Well, it was ridiculous! He was charging her twice what he had said it would be. Well, you know me, Grandma. I couldn't stand it, so I told him – in English – what he had said it would be and then I told him what the total should be. He acted surprised that someone, and just a girl at that, would call him on his deceit. He apologized and apologized and said I was right, and that he had just made a mistake! Then he wrapped up the material and even gave Sookie some thread for free. Then she paid him (with salt) and we left.

When we got home, she told Dog Shoot what had happened. After our night meal he came and got me and we went away from the rest of our group and he talked to me. He said he knew I was sad that the other Indians were ignoring me, but maybe I could get back in their favor by doing their shopping for them. I have never thought that Dog Shoot was especially smart, but he keeps proving me wrong by understanding more than I think he does.

Anyway, he must have talked to the rest of the Cherokees in our camp because the next week, I got a list of things to buy for different groups in our settlement and the money (either salt or real money) to pay for the order.

So, I went to the general store to buy the things on my list. When I got there an Indian was the one to wait on me, so I talked to him in Cherokee (I'm really very good at that tongue). I did all my negotiating with him. When I paid, the store owner came up to me and asked if I was the little girl from last week. I said yes, and we were talking in English. He asked me how well I knew arithmetic. Well, I'm very good at it, and I told him so. He asked how old I was and I told him I was eleven. He asked how I got so smart so I told him about Elizabeth holding school on the wagon train and then after my family got killed I started teaching the Indian children. I found some books in a burned-out schoolhouse and had been using those to teach myself.

Entry 43

He told me there was an Indian school in Tallequah. They only teach Indian children, but maybe I could teach there. I told him I didn't want to do that. (I'll tell you why later, Granny.)

He said that if I didn't want to teach and didn't have a school to go to, he might be interested in giving me a job working for him. I asked him to tell me about the job and here's what he said: I would work from opening to closing six days a week, and I would earn $1.00 a week. I would also eat out of the store for my noon meal. What I would actually do was wait on customers, figure their bills, take their money, and make change.

I asked him why me, and he said it was mostly because I speak both languages really well and I was quick with figures.

After I got all my purchases tied up, I told him I would need to ask Dog Shoot if I could. He asked if Dog Shoot was my guardian. I said, "yes" even though I didn't know what that word meant.

So, I took my purchases and my change and skipped all the way back to camp. When Dog Shoot and I talked tonight he agreed to let me work. I told him I would give him $.50 each week to help pay for my food and because I owed him so much. Anyway, I am excited about having something to do and actually getting paid for it.

Granny, I told you I would explain why I didn't want to teach at the Indian school. The truth is I don't like these Indians up here. They kinda look down on the Texas Cherokees and I consider myself one of them.

The Cherokees who have been here longer say the Texas Cherokees are too much like the white man. They don't like the way we dress or how we live, or even the way we eat. They won't have anything to do with us (kinda like my Indians did when they shunned me – but that's getting better). So, if they don't want us, I don't want to teach in their school. It doesn't matter to me that I'm not even a little bit Cherokee – they were there to take care of me when I needed them and I've thrown in my lot with them.

Also, I looked up "guardian" in the dictionary. It is exactly what Dog Shoot is to me – a protector and provider; one who rears a minor – but not the part about it being a legal thing. That's just what he is. I also told you that the "shunning" (another word I looked up) had gotten a little better. I'm still not welcomed into the little family groups (they are called clans), and some of the Indians act like they are a little afraid of me. Sookie tells me that they are afraid I will bring them bad luck. She said to just be myself and they will come around in time.

Entry 44

Today I started to work. It's great fun and I love it!

I waited on customers (both Indian and white), and ate the noon meal with Mr. Kimbrough (he's the owner) and Slow Foot (he's the employee). When things got slow in the store, I did a little dusting and then began teaching Slow Foot arithmetic. Until now Mr. Kimbrough mostly waited on white people and Slow Foot on the Indians. But Mr. Kimbrough would have to stop what he was doing to figure amounts and money and change for Slow Foot's customers.

I wait on both Indians and whites and handle the money part of it. Mr. Kimbrough watched me real close today but I don't know why. He may have been afraid I would not be honest or that I would need more instructions or would need his help or something.

Mr. Kimbrough has a very good arrangement in the store, and it didn't take me any time to see where the different things were – clothes, foodstuffs, farm implements, etc. So it was easy and fun and the day just flew by.

Mr. Kimbrough told me that I would get paid every Saturday. There's a big calendar on the wall and I can finally keep up with the days, the weeks, the months, and even the year. I don't think I can make you understand how much that has bothered me. Today is Tuesday, November 1, 1839. That's why it is so cold.

Last night I was so excited that I could hardly sleep, but I was very tired. Today has been another good day – Wednesday, November 2, 1839, and something happened at work that was really exciting. Mr. Kimbrough got a shipment of goods on a freight wagon. We (Mr. Kimbrough and I) checked off everything and he paid the man who brought the goods. Then he and I restocked the store with all the new goods. That was fun but the best thing was that I saw a pair of shoes that are perfect. They are made of leather and have laces that go right above the ankle. The heels are about one inch high. I have never seen anything I want so much. They cost $1.00 and after two weeks I'll have enough money to buy them. (Remember I'm giving Dog Shoot $.50 of my pay each week.)

Entry 45

It is getting colder and colder, but I have my new shoes and they really help. It began snowing on November 7 and is still snowing.(It is now the15th.) Every morning I dress up so much that I look like I'm really fat, but I'm not fat at all. I've started making Christmas presents. I thought about buying presents out of my pay, but I want to save my money for something I have in mind, so I'll make presents like I did last Christmas.

When I was back home in Alabama, we made a big deal over Thanksgiving, but the Indians don't seem to celebrate anything. Time is so different to Indians. They don't mark birthdays and so don't know how old they are – and they don't even care! Of course they don't have any idea of Easter or even Christmas.

Mr. Kimbrough talks to me when there are no customers in the store. In one of our conversations we were talking about rotating our schedules so that he could take Mrs. Kimbrough on a little trip. There would have to be two of us in the store at all times. But the point of this story is that while Mr. K. and I were talking, I asked why he called Slow Foot by that name. Mr. Kimbrough burst out laughing and laughed until it looked like he was crying. He said that he wasn't really laughing at me, but that what I said was really funny.

Then he explained that the Indian's name was "Slew Foot," not "Slow Foot" because of the way he walked – with one foot turned funny.

The next day – and that was this morning – I asked Slew Foot what he had done to make his foot sore. He said it wasn't sore, it had just always turned inward all his life. I asked him if it made his growing up years hard – the Indians lay great store by how strong, fast, and tough the boys are. He said it was hard, but he got used to it. Now he has a job and is making money while some of the ones who had teased him are much worse off than he is.

Today something happened at the store that made me happy and may turn out to be important. Over in one corner of the store is a post office. Whenever a stagecoach comes through or even a single rider, they bring letters from wherever they come from. We put the letters in a cubbyhole with the name of the resident of Tallequah on it.

So, sometimes people come in to see if they have mail and I've never seen them before. Well, that happened today. A woman and her daughter, who looked to be about my age, came in. The lady said hello to Mr. Kimbrough and asked if there was any mail for the reverend. Mr. K. looked in a cubbyhole marked "Smith" and got out a letter and gave it to Mrs. Smith. He told her that the last stagecoach had also brought a package for her. While he went in to the back room to find the package, I got to talking with the girl and her mother. It turned out that the girl is named Isabelle. Her daddy is the local preacher.

Isabelle told me that she had seen me pass by on my way to work and back each day. (I'll tell you more about that later.) She asked if I ever had any time off. I told her only on Sunday when the store is closed. Then she and her mother asked me to come to church next Sunday and stay to eat with them. I was so excited, but explained that I would have to ask my guardian. The next day will be Wednesday. I will leave a note at the manse as I pass by, letting her know whether I can come or not.

Entry 46

Let me back up and tell you about my trip to work and back each day. In the morning, I walk to work because the sun is coming up and while it may be cold or wet, or both, it doesn't hurt me to get a little fresh air and exercise, but the evening is a different matter. Every day it gets dark earlier, so Dog Shoot rides in to get me and carries me back home behind him on his horse. It's fun and fast. (Our cabin is about two miles from the store.)

After we ate, I told Dog Shoot I had something important to talk about with him. He and I sat a little apart from the others and I told him what had happened today. He asked me what going to church meant. I told him that there would be a group of people there, but I didn't know if there would be any Indians. Then I told him the people would wear their best clothes and would sing songs and then would listen to the preacher (kinda like a head man) talk to them about something in the Bible.

Since I have a Bible, he didn't ask about that part of it. He wanted to know why I wanted to go. Well, I told him that when I was a little girl in Alabama – before I came to Texas – and when we were in Nacogdoches, I had gone to church every Sunday with my family, and I miss it. He had questions about how I planned to get there and get back home. I had already thought about that and planned to walk. I would be home long before dark. Then he looked straight at me and asked if I really would come back. I guess I embarrassed him because I hugged him around the neck and told him of course I would come back – this is the only family I have and the only home I know outside of Alabama. When I asked if I could go, he said I could.

Entry 47

I left a note at the manse today saying that it would be my pleasure to attend church Sunday and stay to dinner. The rest of the day went by as usual and Dog Shoot was waiting for me when I got off work.

When we got home this evening, Sookie and Wali were excited about something, but it would have to wait until after we ate. Finally we were finished and they showed me what they had been doing all day – making me a new dress! Dog Shoot had told them about my going to church next Sunday and that I needed something to wear. They had used some cloth they had left over from the day Sookie and I first went to Mr. Kimbrough's store. It is blue with little flowers on it. They had made me a skirt that fit perfectly and came down to the tops of my shoes, but they needed me to make the bodice fit right. It will have long sleeves, but not tight ones and a round neck. It will be so pretty and will never have been worn by anybody but me!

Work seemed to drag by today. I'm so excited about getting home to see how my dress is coming along, and I want the time to pass quickly so it will be Sunday (today is Thursday). I told Mr. Kimbrough about my plans for Sunday and he was happy for me – or pretended to be. But I told him I still have one problem – how will I know what time I am supposed to be at the church. He said to let him think about it and he would have an answer tomorrow.

When I got home after work, I was eager to see "my" dress, but Sookie told me I would have to wait until after we ate. It seemed to take forever, but we were finally done. Then Sookie and Wali took me into a corner of the cabin and had me try on my new dress! They had finished it during the day. So I put it on and walked out into the middle of the cabin. Everyone was happy for me. I was so happy that I cried. Then I changed back into my work dress and carefully put my new, blue, church dress away. Then I sat down with Dog Shoot and told him about the problem I had talked to Mr. K. about.

I told you before Granny that Indians have no idea of time and Dog Shoot didn't understand. He said when I get there is when the church should start. I told him that there would be other people coming to church and we wouldn't know when everyone who was coming would be there because of the cold weather and there would be some who just wouldn't come. I tried to explain that church was set for a certain time and everyone who was coming had to be there at that time.

Dog Shoot just wouldn't understand, although it makes perfect sense to me. He kept trying to get me to see that people are the important ones and church should start when the people are there. I tried to get him to see that church is more important than people but he just didn't get it. I guess I do understand his point, but to me church means God and He's certainly more important than anything. Anyway, it's time to go to bed, so I'll just have to see what Mr. Kimbrough says tomorrow.

Well, Mr. Kimbrough had a solution to my question about the time to get to church, but I didn't like it. He said that church would start at ll:00 a.m., but if I got there by 10:30, there would be plenty of time and I would not be nervous. He offered to let me borrow his pocket watch and give it back to him on Monday but there were a couple of reasons I didn't want to do that. First, having such a nice thing would make me uneasy – I might lose it or damage it.

Secondly, Mr. Kimbrough was very proud of his timepiece and he would need it on Sunday himself. Anyway I thanked him kindly, but told him that I would be more nervous if I had it than if I didn't.

After that the day passed smoothly. There were a few customers, but not so many that Slew Foot and I had to miss our arithmetic lesson. Dog Shoot picked me up after work and we rode home to a good supper. After supper I had a little time to work on Christmas presents – mostly things for Wakie and Sally and the new baby to come. I'm making two little look-alike dresses for Wakie and her dolly and a knitted cape for Sally and a matching one for her dolly. Goodnight, dear sweet Granny.

Entry 48

I thought today would never get here, now I think it will never end. It got really cold last night and snowed again. When I got to the store, the first thing I had to do was to take off my shoes and dry them in front of the stove.

There weren't any customers to wait on. It was too cold for anyone to even come in to get their mail. We re-arranged the stock and I dusted. I asked Mr. Kimbrough if he would like for me to put up a Christmas tree in the store and he said he didn't want me to and he told me why. When he was a little boy his daddy always cut a tree and Mr. K. and his mother and sisters decorated it. This particular year, his daddy cut the tree too early, but he just wanted his children to get to enjoy it longer.

Anyway, it dried out something awful and on Christmas Eve it caught fire. It didn't burn the house down, but it burned all their presents and some other stuff in the house. Ever since then his family would decorate in their house, but would not have a tree. So Mr. Kimbrough told me I could make popcorn garlands and things like that and put them in the store but no tree or even pine boughs. So, I'll think about some decorations that won't burn.

Dog Shoot finally got there to take me home. Because it was so cold and we hadn't had any customers, Mr. K. closed a little early — but he still paid me a dollar. We got home a little earlier than usual and I gave Dog Shoot $.50. We finished eating, so I'll work a little more on the girls' Christmas presents and try to get to sleep.

Entry 49

Granny, today was wonderful! I didn't know how much I missed church and talking to people who talk like I do or anything. Let me tell you every little thing that happened. I had doubted that Sunday would ever arrive, but it finally did, after I had waked up several times during the night. Once it was daylight, I helped cook breakfast and made myself eat, although I was so excited that I wasn't the least bit hungry.

After we ate, and I helped clean up the cabin, I very calmly started to get dressed. I knew it was too early to leave, but I couldn't help it! Sookie and Wali helped me to get dressed. It was kind of funny; you would have thought I was getting married or something! After I was dressed and had my shoes on, it was still too early to go, so I just sat down and waited.

Finally it felt like time to leave. I walked slower than I normally do, but eventually I got to the manse, which is right next door to the church. There was no one around, so I was still too early. I tried to stay out of sight, but Mrs. Smith saw me and asked me to come in. I hesitated at first, but she said I could help Isabelle with her hair.

When I went into the house, it was nice and toasty warm. Mrs. Smith had me put my cape and the shawl I had on under it in front of the fireplace in the parlor and put my shoes, too. She offered to let me borrow a pair of Isabelle's house shoes to wear while my shoes dried out and got warm, but I had a pair of little shoes I had knitted in my cape pocket. I take them to work every day to wear at the store so I don't have to keep my wet, cold shoes on all day.

Then Mrs. Smith took me upstairs to Isabelle's room. I know you're curious about the house so I'll tell you a little bit about it. It is a two-story dog trot. One side (the left as you look at it) is the family side and the other side is for church office rooms for the reverend to work in. Upstairs are the bedrooms. There are six of them, but Isabelle is the only child the Smiths have, so they use the other rooms as a guest room and as storage rooms and one as a playroom for Isabelle.

The cookhouse, smoke house, outhouse, and some storage buildings are in the back yard.

When I got to Isabelle's room, it was beautiful! She is directly across from her parents' bedroom at the back of the house and uses the next room toward the front as a playroom. Her bedroom has pretty furniture painted white and a long mirror that sits in a frame on the floor. I just stood and looked at myself in the mirror for a long time! My blue dress is really pretty and fits good, too. Instead of me helping Isabelle with her hair, she loaned me some blue ribbons for mine and even tied bows for me in them.

We talked and played a while and then Mrs. Smith called us to go to Sunday school.

Granny, I either had forgotten or had never known how wonderful it is to have a girl friend.

Entry 50

Mrs. Smith taught our Sunday school class, I guess because her daughter was in there. There were two other girls in the class that day, but I didn't pay much attention to them, my thoughts were all on Mrs. Smith and Isabelle. We heard the story of Jonah and the whale. It's funny that Jonah thought he could run away from the Lord and then got mad because God forgave the Ninevites.

Anyway, after Sunday school, we all met together in a large room and visited and drank hot chocolate. Isabelle said that when it wasn't snowing or not so cold, we would go outside between Sunday school and church. While we were in the "fellowship hall," I met all the people near my age. The two girls from Sunday school are both younger than Isabelle and me. There are two boys, one our age and one a little older.

All the people at church are white and live in the town. Isabelle said the Indians go to their own church. Several people asked me questions about myself, but I was able to avoid telling them anything really.

Then we all went in to church.

Rev. Smith preached about God being with us everywhere. It all tied in with the Sunday school lesson. But the best part was the singing! Mrs. Smith played the piano and we sang some songs that I already knew and remembered from Alabama.

When the service was over, Mr. and Mrs. Smith, Isabelle, and I walked over to the manse. The Smiths have only two slaves – a woman who takes care of everything in the house and her husband. I guess he does things outside, but he helps in the house, too. Again, it was just like Alabama –the slaves work all day Sunday until their owners are through with dinner, then they are able to go to their church.

Dinner was great: We had fried chicken and mashed potatoes and gravy and biscuits. Then we had peach cobbler for dessert. The peaches had been canned and were in the root cellar, or so Mrs. Smith said. It was the best food I had had since, well, in a long time.

Entry 51

As if that weren't enough, after we ate, Mr. Smith asked me to come in his office. He said that he did not want to pry, but he was very curious about me. I could certainly understand that. Here I was, a blond-haired, green-eyed American girl living with Indians and speaking their language like a native – with no sign of any other American around. So I told him all about you and about our coming to Texas from Talladega. We found a good place to live, but then that horrible October day in 1838, renegades massacred my mother's family. The only way I escaped was that I was away from home picking grapes. Then I told him how the Cherokee Indians rescued me and the big chief adopted me as his granddaughter and took real good care of me.

Rev. Smith asked me if there was any way he could help me. I said I was so happy that he had a daughter – that I am happier than I have been since I lost my family. Just going to a Cumberland church again and singing songs that I have heard before and making friends with other young people, especially Isabelle, means more to me than I ever would have thought possible.

Rev. Smith was so nice to me – he said that if I wanted, he would make sure that I was a part of all the young people's activities. I said, "Sure," and I promised to come to Sunday school and church every time I can.

By this time Dog Shoot was waiting for me in the yard, so I thanked my hosts and got my cape and shoes on and went out in the yard to ride home with Dog Shoot. I chattered all the way home and the time passed quickly – I didn't even have time to feel the cold.

When we got home, everyone wanted to hear about my Sunday. There was a big pot of stew on the fire and until suppertime we talked about my day. I was careful to make a big fuss about how everyone liked my dress – and that was true; they really did.

Then it was time for supper. I noticed that Dog Shoot didn't have much to say. I thought it was because the rest of us were talking so much. But that wasn't it. After we ate, I moved over beside Dog Shoot and asked if everything was o.k. He didn't answer for a minute and then looked me in the eye and said he was worried. I asked if he was worried about Wali and the expected baby, but he said, "No." He was worried about me. About me! I'm happier than I have been in a long time – what's to worry about! Well, here's how Dog Shoot looks at it. He said he knew I was happy now that I am around white people again, and he is afraid that I want to go back to the white people – to live with them and be one of them again.

I tried to explain that I love being with the Indians and being one of them. I wouldn't change my life now for anything, but I said I really didn't know if the Indians wanted to keep me. Dog Shoot really isn't too good at explaining how he feels, but he thinks he has an obligation to take care of me because of Duwali – but it has grown to be more than that.

Dog Shoot said that all the Indians in our cabin have come to accept me as part of he family – and an important part at that. That almost made me cry. I asked about how he felt about me and he shrugged and said, "You're my little sister," and then I really did cry. When I got over my crying spell, I asked if I could keep on being friends with Isabelle and he said, "Yes." I told him I didn't want to feel guilty about having friends besides the Indians, but I would give them up if he thought I should.

He said I could keep my family and my friends – as long as I remembered who my family is – meaning the Indians.

I was so tired that night that I fell asleep while I was writing in my journal.

Entry 52

I guess Indians feel the same way about weather as they do about time. They don't think about someone's age or birthday or anything like that. Back home in Alabama – and even in our home in Texas -- we had a big thermometer hanging on the porch that kept us aware of the temperature. The Indians are much more casual about the heat or as it is now, the cold. All that matters to them is the season – time to plant, to harvest, etc. What all this has to do with anything is that this winter is the coldest I've ever seen.

And it's not just me; everyone who makes it in to the store says the same thing. I try to go to work every day, even though Mr. Kimbrough has told me time after time that I don't have to. But every day I make it in to work, both Mr. K and Slew Foot are there. Going to work gives me something meaningful to do and helps me feel like a responsible person. Everybody in my family -- families – has always worked and I can't imagine not. This is not to say the others don't do their parts -- they do. We all have different parts to play and different abilities.

Some great news today! It was bitterly cold, but there was no sleet or snow, just beautiful, sparkling sunshine. Mrs. Smith and Isabelle made their way to the store – to see me! Mrs. Smith said her family was so tired of staying inside during the cold weather that they had decided to have a party at the manse on Friday night. Isabelle asked (really begged) me to come to the party and spend the night with her. All the girls at the party are being asked to spend the night. Because it is so cold, Rev. Smith will take the boys home in a wagon (I don't know how they'll get to the Smiths).

I thanked both Mrs. Smith and Isabelle and told them if my guardian said "yes," I would certainly be there. I don't know what Dog Shoot will stay about my spending the night. It will be the first night I've stayed away from home (any of my homes) since we left Alabama, and then I only occasionally stayed with my cousins or some other family member. I don't know why I'm telling you this; you were one of the ones I spent the night with. Anyway, I'm excited, but just a little bit nervous.

As usual, Mr. K. let me go home as soon as Dog Shoot got there and by the time we got to the cabin, it was nearly dark, but it wasn't late. We went in and ate before it got too dark to see. When we were through I told Dog Shoot I wanted to talk to him. We sat a little apart from everyone else and I told him about the party. I asked him if Indians ever had parties, and he smiled and said yes, they did. He thought about it a while and finally agreed to let me go. I'll leave a note at the manse tomorrow as I go to work.

Something really good happened at work on Thursday. I had told Mr. K. on Wednesday that I would come to work on Friday and would bring my party dress with me. Then, after work I would change clothes at the Smiths and stay there for the party and spend the night. Then I would change back into work clothes and come to work Saturday. Well, on Thursday Mr. Kimbrough said he had something for me. I asked if it was a Christmas present, and he said, "no, it was a 'just because' gift." Then he gave me a carpetbag! They come in two sizes (at least at Mr. K's store) large and small. He gave me a small one made from a beautiful piece of heavy cloth. It looked like a real lady's bag and I felt guilty about taking it. Mr. K. asked me how many carpetbags we had sold since I went to work for him – well, actually none – and when I told him so, he said,

"Well, see." I didn't really know what he meant by that, but I was thrilled with the gift. I kinda wanted it to be a Christmas present, but what Mr. K. says, goes.

When Dog Shoot picked me up to go home, he was impressed with the bag also. Then when we got home, everyone else (except Chooch) was, too.

Entry 53

So, Friday morning I carefully folded my blue dress and my nightdress and put them in my new bag. Then, wearing my work dress and my boots, Dog Shoot took me to work. You would have thought that I was leaving on a long journey instead of just two miles for two days. Everyone (except Chooch) kissed me goodbye and told me they would miss me. However, when we got to the store, it was a different story. It suddenly dawned on me that this will be the longest I've gone without seeing my Indian family. Dog Shoot asked again if I was sure I would be coming back. I said, "Of course." Then I embarrassed him by kissing him on the check.

The day dragged by so slowly that I thought it would never be over. But finally it was and I ran down to Isabelle's house (it's pretty close by). There I put my shoes by the fire and went to eat with the Smiths. After supper, Isabelle and I went upstairs to her room to change clothes. By that time my shoes were toasty warm and I put them back on.

Isabelle really was excited by my new carpetbag and even showed it to her mother. I bet her mother and daddy will give her one for Christmas – it's only a couple of weeks away.

After we dressed and fixed our hair, we went downstairs to greet the other guests. The parents had all come to bring their children and stayed a while.

One really good thing about the young people's party (they call it a play party) was the music. There was a piano, which Mrs. Smith played, and the outdoor slave played a fiddle. We did round dances to the music. All I had ever seen were square dances, but these were easy and fun. There were plenty of people (mostly the girls) to teach you the steps. Some of the girls showed us all new steps and we had fun learning them.

When we were tired from the dancing, we went from the parlor into the dining room to have punch and little cakes. It was just too lovely!

I wished the party could go on forever, but after a while Mr. Smith had his slave bring the wagon around and all the boys got ready to go home. Their parents had left right after the punch and cake. After their parents left, the young people broke into pairs or small groups and just talked and acted silly – at least the boys did and the girls laughed at them, and that just made them act sillier.

After Mr. Smith had loaded up the boys and left to take them home, Isabelle and the rest of the girls went upstairs. The house slave had made us pallets on the playroom floor. Although it was bitterly cold outside, it was warm enough for sleeping upstairs. One of my books said that hot air rises and it did.

It was fun being with all the girls. We experimented with twisting our hair up and talked about how we would wear it when we were older. After we got on our pallets, we did the funnest thing – maybe I shouldn't admit to this, but we practiced kissing! Not each other, but our hands. I guess we were all pretending it was a beau, but nobody seemed to pretend it was one of the boys at the party! When we finally went to sleep, I imagine we all dreamed about our particular knight in shining armor.

Entry 54

Saturday morning we got up and got dressed and had breakfast, then Rev. Smith began taking the girls home in the wagon. He dropped me off at the store because Mr. K. and Slew Foot were already there and there was smoke coming out of the chimney pipe.

Mr. K. wanted to know about the grownups at the party. He didn't ask about the young people — either he didn't care or he was being polite.

It was so cold that we only had a couple of customers and they didn't buy much. Most people are eating out of their smokehouses as much as they can.

When it finally got to be time to go home, Dog Shoot was waiting for me as usual. He almost smiled when he saw me – a first time for that. It was getting colder all the time and by the time we got home it was starting to snow. Of course, I had to tell everything about my night at the party.

I finally got a good night's sleep, but I woke up to a new snowfall. It was too cold to go to church. I felt really bad about not going since I had just gone to the party at the manse.

It turned out that Sunday wasn't the only day we had to stay in because of the cold. I worked on Christmas presents all day Monday and part of Tuesday. On Wednesday I insisted on going to work. It wasn't snowing but the snow was deep and it was slow going but I finally reached the store about the middle of the morning. Mr. Kimbrough and Slew Foot were both there and Mr. K. had a pot of soup bubbling on the stove. We didn't have any customers all day so Mr. K. and I rearranged the stock, which has really gotten down low. It's been a long time since a shipment got through. There haven't been any stagecoaches or riders either, so there's no new mail.

Dog Shoot came to get me about 4:30 (I could tell that because of the clock on the wall, but of course, Dog Shoot couldn't). I forgot to mention that Slew Foot and I are continuing our lessons every day that business is slow. He's pretty good at arithmetic and so he's learning to tell time now. Also, when it's slow, all three of us play dominos. It's fun and makes the time pass.

It's just a week until Christmas and it's awfully cold. I never knew it could be so cold – it certainly wasn't in Talledega or even in Texas. I don't know if it's this cold in all of the Indian Territory, but it's too cold for me! I have all my Christmas presents finished and am spending my spare time doing several things: I'm helping Sookie cook and learning a little bit more about that. Also I'm reading some in my books, and I'm doing some knitting, mostly covers for the beds. With it so cold, we can never have enough covers.

Chooch is kept busy gathering wood for the fire. He and Dog Shoot have to go farther and farther to find dead wood. Dog Shoot says that in the spring the two of them will cut some live trees and stack the wood to dry out for next winter.

Entry 55

I found out something that I never knew before, but I should have figured it out. You see, Grandma, the most important thing in the Indians' life is the clan. I already told you that the mothers raise their boys until they are about the age that I am now, then the men of the mother's clan (or family) raise him on to adulthood. It turns out that Dog Shoot and Sookie are brother and sister – so Dog Shoot is supposed to be teaching Chooch—I just didn't realize that was what he was doing or why. I guess I didn't recognize Dog Shoot's teaching because he is so easy about it. It's totally different from the way I teach or even how Sookie teaches me. In both those cases we give instructions, let whoever we are teaching practice and then keep on going back over the lessons.

Dog Shoot just tells Chooch to do something and expects him to do it. Most of the time Dog Shoot goes with Chooch, but he seems to be just watching.

I haven't been to work since last Wednesday. Now it looks like I won't get back until after Christmas. It's so bitterly cold that we don't even want to stick our noses outside! Christmas will be Friday and today is Wednesday.

Wali doesn't feel well and spent most of today in bed. Sookie did all the cooking today because I was busy with the younger children. In case you don't remember them all, I'll name them again for you. Of course there's Chooch, but he's about 16 and not a kid at all. He has a little sister named Sally, but she's a little slow and doesn't do much except sit by herself and play with her doll. One day I asked Sookie about her because she didn't seem able to learn like the other kids. Sookie said not to worry about her. As long as she was happy and nobody picked on her, she would be o.k. Of course, Chooch keeps an eye on her and no one had better tease her when he's around.

The next child is Wakie. She's about 6 or 7 years old now and is the daughter of Sam Benge and Wali. Now that Wali and Dog Shoot are married, he is Wakie's daddy and very soon they will have their own baby.

So this means Dog Shoot is the grown man in our little family and Chooch is next. Everybody else is a woman or girl: Sookie and Sally, Wali and Wakie, and me.

Entry 56

Now it's Christmas Eve and I still can't get in to work because of the cold. I'll bet the snow is two feet deep and the temperature – well I don't know how cold it is – just too cold! I feel terrible about missing work, but I feel even worse when I try to go outside. This afternoon Wali started feeling worse and worse. Sookie hung around her and so did Quatie. Dog Shoot, Chooch, and I kept the children occupied. I told all the Christmas stories I could think of and sang every Christmas song I ever heard. By the end of the day, everybody was singing them, too.

It's finally Christmas morning! We received the best gift ever last night – or rather early in the morning. Wali had her and Dog Shoot's little boy before dawn. I asked what they were going to name him and Dog Shoot just said, "Not yet." I don't really know when he will get a name or who will name him, but that's not important right now. I just call him "Baby" and he's beautiful!

All we did today was hold the baby. When it got to be time to eat supper, I gave everyone their presents. Then I told the Christmas story while holding the baby! It was so beautiful that I nearly cried.

Dog Shoot is so proud. He holds that baby so gently, like he's afraid he will drop him or break him!

The weather finally heated up today (it's Saturday). The snow started melting but I still did not go to work; however, I definitely will on Monday if the weather holds. Something elso good happened today. Mr. Kimbrough and Slew Foot came riding up this afternoon. They had each brought me a Christmas present. Mr. Kimbrough gave me several skeins of beautiful yarn and Slew Foot had carved me a flute. He showed me how to play it, and it is really pretty easy. Then they admired the new baby before they rode back to town. I just seem to want to look at the baby and hold him, but I need to get back in my routine. It's nice to hang around the cabin and play, but I feel guilty. I'm supposed to be working, not just lazing around.

Today is Sunday. Since the weather's not too awful, I'm going to church. It's the first time I've been since the party at Isabelle's. I wrapped up, put my warm slippers in my pocket (I think I forgot to tell you that I made slippers for everyone in the cabin, even the baby and the little girls' dolls), and wore my work dress. It's brown and pretty dull, but it's warmer than my blue dress.

Once I got to church, I put my boots by the fire. They were too big when I got them, but my feet have grown and they are about to get a little tight.

It was so good to see my white friends, to have a Sunday school lesson, to eat white food, to hear a real sermon, and to sing familiar songs. Everybody who was at the party at the manse was in church. So I got to visit with everybody and told all about the new baby. When someone asked what the baby was to me, I said I guess he is my nephew. Dog Shoot called me his little sister, so I would be the baby's aunt. When I was back in Alabama with you Granny, I remember the women talking about family and how everybody was related to each other. Of course, I didn't join in, I just played with my cousins and my doll, but I listened. I guess I was one of those little pitchers with big ears that you were always talking about.

After Church I was glad to get back home to see the baby. Mrs. Smith invited me to eat with them, but I told her I couldn't. When I got home, I held the baby and talked to him about being his aunt. The rest of the day was just like any other day – reading, playing with the little girls and practicing on my flute.

Entry 57

Monday at last and I'm going back to work. I rode into work with Dog Shoot as usual. He let me off and told me he would be back to get me this afternoon.

We had a couple of customers today, but they were mostly interested in the mail, which we didn't have. I suspect they wanted to get out of their houses just like I did. Mr. Kimbrough says that if the weather stays warm, we will soon get mail and maybe even some supplies that we ordered a long time ago. We will really be busy then. About 4:30 Dog Shoot showed up with his Christmas present for me. It is a cute little pony, and it even looks like his horse. It is a pinto with brown spots. It's obvious though that they are two different kinds of animal. Dog Shoot's horse is tall with long legs and mine is a short, kinda chubby pony. I rode my pony (I'm going to call him "Lucky") home next to Dog Shoot. I was so excited – first the baby and now my very own pony!

Wali is doing very well. She stayed in bed the first day and slept except when she was feeding the baby. Now she's up and taking care of the baby – when she can get him away from the little girls long enough. After we have finished eating supper, Dog Shoot sits and holds their baby and just looks at him. Wali sings Indian songs to him and I sing songs in English. I was around babies enough in Alabama that I heard plenty of little songs and can remember most of them. I'm also learning to play these songs on my new flute.

Things are getting back in a routine. The New Year begins tomorrow and the thaw has continued. It is still very cold, but we've had no new snow or ice since before Christmas.

So, I've ridden Lucky to work every day. The baby is getting along nicely and Wali feels good again.

Finally the supply wagon has gotten through – and it brought the mail with it. Mr. Kimbrough put me to work putting the mail up while he put up, or put out, the stock. Several people came in for their mail; almost no one stayed for the goods, but they mostly promised to come back later to look at all we will have for sale.

Entry 58

It's now about the middle of January and the cold has set in again. It stayed a little warmer just long enough for the church to have a watch night party. Of course I had to explain to the Indians what that is. They must think white people are crazy. To watch for the New Year is crazy to them because they do not recognize years or months or days.

Anyway, right after the watch party, it turned bitterly cold again and so that ended my church going for a while. Something strange and a little bit scary happened today and it made a lot of other things happen. First, when I go to work (most days), I ride Lucky and go by myself. So, anyway, I rode in and put Lucky in the barn and went into the store to work. A couple of white men came in and looked all around the store. I felt a little uneasy and sent Slew Foot into the back to get Mr. K. When he came to the front he sent me back to work in the storeroom and told me not to come back until he called me.

Since I was in the back I didn't know what was going on until he called me out of the back room to come eat with him and Slew Foot. As we ate, he told me that the two men were more interested in me than in the merchandise. He didn't know who they were, but when I told him about the three men who kidnapped Alcey and Ancih and killed Ancih, he said it was possible these two men were the two who got away, and they might still be thinking about kidnapping me for ransom.

Anyway he closed the store early that day and both he and Slew Foot rode home with me. When we got there, the men sent me inside and put Lucky up or me and then talked a long time with Dog Shoot. I didn't hear what they were saying, but of course I knew. Then when Dog Shoot came in to eat, he didn't say anything about it.

The next morning I saw the results of that talk Dog Shoot had with Mr. Kimbrough. When I went out to get Lucky, Dog Shoot was already there. Then that and every day he rode with me to the store and was there to pick me up in time to get home before dark – and he always had his rifle with him.

After this had gone on a few days, I finally got him to talk (and to listen) to me. I told him I felt bad about taking up all his time just escorting me to and from work when he could be doing something useful. He told me that he had promised Duwali that he would take care of me and protect me and that's what he intended to do. Of course, there was no arguing with him or with Duwali's orders.

Entry 59

For the past month Dog Shoot has been like a shadow to me. I have been to church twice, with Dog Shoot escorting me both there and back. I had a long talk with Rev. Smith between Sunday school and church explaining why I wasn't around so much. He said he thought it was wise for others to look out for me. He said he had heard of the two men who were I town, but that no one knew them or what they wanted, but that they made everyone feel uneasy. He also told me not to worry if I could not make it to church; he would understand.

Granny, on the days I don't write in my journal, it's because nothing has happened. It's getting on toward spring, and I don't know what the arrangement will be then for my going to work. Dog Shoot and Chooch will have work to do and can't spend the time to take me to and from work. They'll be working then and making some money, so maybe I won't need to work. But Mr. K. will need me more than ever, what with farming beginning and seeds and implements to sell.

Well, it's been a few days since I wrote and I have part of the answer to "what happens next?" Last Sunday it was dark and stormy all day. We stayed in the cabin all day and I rearranged my belongings again. My satchel is getting pretty worn, so I put all the loose papers and pencils in there. Then I arranged all my books, of which I have quite a few now – my Bible, my journals, my schoolbooks, and some other favorites of mine – in my carpet bag. It's not only fat, but also heavy. Anyway I am glad I did because of what happened that same day.

It was the middle of the afternoon when it suddenly got as dark as night. Dog Shoot told us to all get what we could carry in one trip and get into the root cellar. He and Chooch went to turn out the livestock and then got their guns and met us in the cellar. We bolted the door from the inside and waited. While we waited, I asked everybody what they had brought down with them. (As much to keep our minds off what might be going on outside as anything.) The women, except me, had brought clothing and blankets and practical things. The children brought their favorite toys and the men brought their guns and ammunition.

You know what I brought – my satchel and my carpetbag. Dog Shoot and Chooch laughed at me but said they weren't surprised. I had just started to tell them that I had brought what I treasured most in the world, when suddenly we heard a loud roaring and then it sounded as if all the angels in heaven were having a battle against the forces of the Devil. Since then John Milton's *Paradise Lost*, one of my favorite books and one in my carpetbag, has been a lot clearer to me.

Finally the noises from outside died down. Dog Shoot would not let us go outside in case the storm was not over and we finally all fell asleep in that dank, cold, and dark place.

Entry 60

The next morning we found that we couldn't get out! There was something laying across the cellar door that would not let us get the door open. We all pushed and worked on the door without making any progress until we heard some yelling on the other side. After a while, the weight (it was a tree) was removed from the door and it was pulled open.

There was Mr. Kimbrough and Rev. Smith, and some of our neighbors who came from Texas with us. When we got out of there, all we could see was devastation. Our house was gone, as well as the barn. The only things left were the smokehouse and us. We thanked and thanked our rescuers who told us we had the worst of the storm. All the time, I was looking for some sign of the animals.

The day was beautiful now, so we built a fire in the old fireplace of our cabin and ate from the smokehouse. Our rescuers were too polite to eat our food. They knew it would have to last us for a long time.

After Mr. Kimbrough and Rev. Smith and the others left, we picked through the rubble for anything that might have escaped the storm and its winds. It didn't really hit me just what we had lost until I saw a piece of material up in a tree – the material my party dress was made from. That's when I started crying and could not stop. I cried for all the people I have lost from my Williams family through Ancih. Everyone tried to comfort me, but it did little to help until I started crying for Lucky and Dog Shoot's horse. Then I heard a commotion behind me and when I turned around I saw Chooch coming out of the woods with the two horses. I think Dog Shoot was just as happy as I was, but whatever, I stopped crying immediately.

Then after we ate I sat by Lucky stroking him and telling him how lucky we all were to be alive and to have saved all the things most dear to us. We'll just have to wait and see what comes next.

The storm was Sunday and we spent Monday, Tuesday, and Wednesday doing what we could. We have had plenty of practice sleeping on the ground and having a campfire for cooking and for light, so it wasn't too hard. However, Dog Shoot is thoroughly fed up with this place and wants to move us somewhere else – he just doesn't know where.

On Thursday I rode in to work with Chooch keeping me company – and carrying a rifle. When we got to the store, he told me he would be back for me after work and galloped away.

Entry 61

Mr. Kimbrough was surprised to see me. I guess Slew Foot was too, but he's an Indian and doesn't show his feelings, but that's another thing I am used to. Mr. Kimbrough was so kind to me. He asked if there was anything at all in the store that I needed and that I could have it. He was proud that I have saved my carpetbag that he had given me. He also asked about foodstuffs and even pots and pans.

As we were eating at noon, I told him what Dog Shoot had said – that he wanted us to move away. I explained that we had never had such a cold winter and certainly no storm like the one on Sunday. There was another reason too that I told him about. I explained that the other Cherokees did not like us; that they thought the Texas Cherokees were too much like the white man. Mr. K. didn't laugh, but I think he wanted to – after all, I am white, but I don't always think of myself that way.

I told Mr. Kimbrough that there wasn't anywhere else to go. The government wouldn't let us go back to Texas and the Choctaws had only tolerated us for a while. As we talked, I told him that we were treated o.k. by the people (soldiers and their families) at Fort Towson. Mr. Kimbrough said to let him think about it and he might have a solution for us. He asked that I have Dog Shoot bring me to work tomorrow and he would talk to him. Chooch showed up about the middle of the afternoon and Mr. Kimbrough sent me home with him.

I miss the cabin but the women had found some more of the furnishings farther in the woods than where we had looked for three days. I asked Dog Shoot to come to work with me the next day because Mr. Kimbrough wanted to talk with him.

Dog Shoot did accompany me to work this morning. He and Mr. Kimbrough went into the back room and talked most of the morning. News of the storm destroying our house had gotten around town. Soon Slew Foot and I had a steady stream of customers. Not so much to buy as to talk about the storm (twister, they called it and that fit how it treated our things.)

Shortly after Dog Shoot left, the three of us had our noon meal and Mr. Kimbrough explained what he and Dog Shoot had talked about. It surprised me that Mr. Kimbrough agreed that we should leave, but in addition to the reasons I gave him yesterday, he brought up the feeling we all had that the men who were in the store that day might want to kidnap me.

Mr. Kimbrough said that he had gone over last night and talked to Rev. Smith and they agreed that the soldiers at Fort Towson were there to look after all the Indians; to keep them from crossing the river into Texas and in general to protect them. Mr. Kimbrough and Rev. Smith were of the opinion that if were to go to the fort and ask for protection, they would give it to us. Of course, we would have to tell them the whole story of our troubles we have faced and maybe even offer to work for them somehow and to follow their rules just until we could find some other solution. Rev. Smith offered to write a letter for us to take to the head man at Towson and he would ask him to look out for us for a while.

Entry 62

When Dog Shoot showed up to get me, he told Mr. Kimbrough that we would follow his suggestions and that we would leave in just a few days.

The next couple of days were spent getting ready to move. I didn't get to church on Sunday, but that afternoon church came to me! Soon after our noon meal on Sunday, Rev. and Mrs. Smith, Isabelle and some of the people from the church—young and old alike—showed up. They had brought gifts of clothes, kitchen goods, and even some yarn for me! Mrs. Smith told us to take everything we could use, even if it had been used before because it was still good and usable. I laughed and told her that my shoes and the blue dress I wore to the first party at her house were the first things that I had ever had that weren't "hand-me-downs."

Mr. Kimbrough was with them and had a special present for me—another pair of shoes. I have just about outgrown my first pair. He is such a dear, dear man. I hugged him tight and told him that I would never forget him. He assured me that he would never forget me either.

Dog Shoot's plan is for us to leave first thing in the morning. Several other Texas Cherokees are going part of the way with us. They plan to move to some other place in the Cherokee Territory, and will drop out of our wagon train when they find a place that suits them.

After we got on the way, another good thing happened. Slew Foot came galloping up to say good-bye to me!

It really made me feel good. He brought me a flute to remember him by. I don't know if it is the same one he had given me for Christmas and he had looked until he found it, or if he carved me another one. Either way, it was nice of him and good to see him one last time.

Entry 63

I have to tell you, Granny, that the trip back south was totally unlike the one north to Tallequah. Actually, I was a little bit glad to be bored for a change. Of course, you know me, I'm never really bored. I have all sorts of new clothes and even new shoes to try on whenever we stopped – usually only at night. Mostly I walk along side of the wagons and talk with the others who are walking. The only ones who ride in the wagons are very young children, or old, or sick people. At night I often knit or just visit around the campfire.

There is one thing I want to talk to you about when I see you and that is illness. I've never been sick a day in my life (that I remember), but now Dog Shoot is sick and I'm really worried about him. He has a cough and runs out of breath some times. He isn't even old. He's fully gown up and is probably closer in age to my daddy than he is to my brothers. Every night I pray for him to get well, but so far he keeps on coughing. Everyone else is doing fine. The baby is growing and getting strong.

They have named the baby Sam (after Sam Benge), but Dog Shoot says that is his white name. When he gets older (I guess a teenager) a holy man will tell him his real – Indian – name. Even then, he will still be called Sam.

It seems that only he and the holy man will know his real name. Then Dog Shoot started coughing and went to bed. Today we lost three families. I guess they are all related somehow. We came up on a beautiful place. It had a spring to supply water, and trees, a nice slight rise in the ground from the water and the men spent a long time checking out the soil, even tasting it, until they decided it would be a good, fertile place to live. There are big hills (or mountains) off in the distance, but it's pretty flat here. We'll continue our journey south tomorrow.

Well, this morning the other two families traveling with us decided to stay in this place also. Now, it's just our little family continuing south. I think we're close to Choctaw Territory. We're all a little nervous about that, I just hope the first Choctaws we run into will be as kind as the earlier ones were the first time we came through their territory.

Entry 64

We are now a good two days into the Choctaw land and are following a roadway, hoping it will take us to the fort, or at least near it.

We finally saw some Choctaws. At first a couple of men on horses saw us and rode away. Then they came back with an older Indian – I guess he's their headman. He and Dog Shoot talked – some in English, a little in Cherokee, and some sign language. When they got through talking Dog Shoot told us that we were going on to Fort Towson, but it would cost us the last of our salt. The Choctaw did tell Dog Shoot the quickest way to get to the fort and we should be there in two more days.

We traveled all day yesterday and arrived at the fort late in the afternoon today. Before we were allowed to go into the fort, the Choctaw took the rest of our salt from Dog Shoot. Salt, of course, is the most precious thing we own. Without it, we could not preserve any meat or fish. We don't have a place for a smokehouse, and we haven't been in one place long enough to smoke anything.

When we got into the fort, we all waited in the wagon while Dog Shoot went into a cabin to talk with the headman and to give him the letters from Reverend Smith and Mr. Kimbrough. He was in there a long, long time. We were all pretty hungry by this time and those of us who were old enough were pretty worried, too. I don't know what we'll do if the soldiers don't let us stay. We don't have anywhere else to go.

When Dog Shoot finally came back, he said everything was o.k. A soldier led us to a place outside the fort grounds and kinda behind the fort. The women fixed something to eat while the men prepared a place for us to sleep. After we ate, we sat around our campfire and Dog Shoot told us what had happened in the cabin. It took him a long time, what with having to stop to cough and he was very tired. Basically, this is what happened: first of all the headman is a Colonel Loomis. He read the letters Dog Shoot brought him and then had Dog Shoot tell him our whole story, starting with Sam Benge's settlement. The colonel asked questions until he had the whole story – at least as far as it happened after I became part of their family. It was getting late and we were all tired, so Dog Shoot told us to get to sleep and he would tell us the rest in the morning.

Here's what happened today. We got up and had something to eat. After we ate, Dog Shoot told us that the reason the soldiers were willing to let us stay on at the fort is that I was (or am) a white person and an American citizen. What the two of them worked out was that Dog Shoot would be in charge of getting salt out of the soil, using the method they used at Sam Benge's place in Texas and he will teach the Choctaws how to do it. Dog Shoot and Chooch will build us a cabin and we will have a garden place. The only thing that the Cherokees (and I) cannot do is leave the fort compound.

Dog Shoot and Chooch began chopping down trees to build our cabin. Chooch has to do most of the work because Dog Shoot just can't. Chooch is more than able to handle this job. I'm really getting to admire him.

Entry 65

Colonel Loomis assigned an enlisted man (instead of an officer) to show me around the fort. The fort property is U-shaped. The closed end is where the administration offices are, as well as quarters for Col. Loomis and his family and also quarters for the colonel's main two officers and their families. Along the west side are a storeroom, a laundry and a school, and two barracks for enlisted men.

The eastern leg of the fort contains another storeroom, a jail, and two more barracks for enlisted men. All these buildings are built on high foundations of stone. On top of these foundations are cabins painted a pretty sky blue. The foundations are so tall because there is a large creek to the north and the Red River is to the southwest. That's the river we crossed when we first came into Indian Territory. My soldier-guide told me that they have pretty bad floods here ever so often.

The open part of the U is the parade ground where the soldiers practice their drills every day. There is also a flagpole in front of the administration offices and the soldiers raise the flag every morning and lower it each evening. It's pretty impressive, with a bugler playing and all.

The rest of the buildings are outside the U. These include a hospital, the post commissary (what we would call a general store) with a post office included, a blacksmith shop, a bakeshop, the stables and a carpenter shop. Just a little behind these are cabins for people who live here but are not Choctaws. Besides our cabin, there is one for the doctor, one for the teacher, etc. There are a few families of some of the enlisted men. When the enlisted men are assigned to the fort, their families may come with them, but the government does not pay for their housing and the men still have to live in the barracks. In all, it's quite a town. The Choctaws do not live here but come into town (or the fort) to buy things, to get disputes settled by the colonel, or to see the doctor. Things like that. I don't know where they get their money, but I would think they barter for the things they need.

There is one other thing I haven't told you about and that is the roads. There are two big roads that come in to Fort Towson from two other forts. The one to the northeast goes to Fort Smith and the one to the southeast leads to Fort Jesup. The soldier who showed me around said the army built the roads to connect military forts. He said he supposed other forts had roads to them also, but he really didn't know. I asked who used the roads besides armies and he said that is where the stagecoaches run and how the mail gets to us.

Entry 66

Granny, I know you are curious about everything so I'll tell you how our days are spent. It is summer now and it was a wet spring, so there's plenty of salt to be gotten out of the ground, so Dog Shoot and Chooch, along with Sookie and Wali go to the salt grounds. I watch little Sammy and Wakie and Sally. Sally is old enough to be a lot of help. After I clean the cabin, I cook lunch and everybody comes home for lunch. After lunch is naptime for the children and for Dog Shoot.

I don't know where Chooch goes, but I often spend the afternoons visiting the bakery (where I learn a little more about cooking), or visiting with the teacher where she lets me help some of the slower children, or – best of all -- I go to the sewing circle, as the older women call it. I help teach there, too, but most of the women already know how to knit or crochet. I have learned quite a bit about making dresses and I have made one beautiful one and am working on another. It's something I really enjoy.

The only cloud in my life now is Dog Shoot's health. He coughs all the time now and is very short of breath. The doctor at the fort comes to see him regularly and often. The doctor doesn't tell me much – he reports to Dog Shoot's wife. I can tell though that he isn't going to live much longer.

I had been visiting neighbors most of the afternoon today and came back to the cabin to find Dog Shoot failing fast. The doctor arrived late that evening and said that he would stay the night. This was not welcome news to me. I thought it meant Dog Shoot was very sick indeed. Late that night I heard the last sound I wanted to hear – keening by the women in our cabin. I didn't need anyone to tell me what that meant. I got out of bed, wrapped a blanket around myself and went to find Sookie and Wali. I found that keening is something that seems to come quite naturally.

Today there has been much to do. The colonel came to see us and asked if we planned to make any changes in our living arrangements. We told him it was too early to say but we would let him know just as soon as we had discussed it and made some decisions.

The Indians had a traditional burial here at the Fort Towson graveyard. After Dog Shoot was buried, we put rocks on his grave. We made it look as good as we could and Chooch made a wooden cross to put at the head of the grave. This wasn't something that they would naturally do, but I asked Chooch to do it and he did.

We went back to the cabin and talked about our future. Sookie said that she and Chooch and Sally would go to the place where our group broke up and they would stay there until they could locate some other members of their clan. Wali and Wakie and little Sam would go with them until they could find where the rest of Wali's family is living. So that just leaves me. I'm o.k. with being here, but I can understand how they would want to get out of this foreign land among Indians who don't want them here and find their own families. Even Col. Loomis is worried about the Cherokees. He is as kind as can be to me, but he's not quite as accepting of the Cherokees.

Entry 67

Sookie gave me all the money I had given to Dog Shoot when I was working at Mr. Kimbrough's store. I didn't want to take it because I can always make money, but Sookie said that Dog Shoot always intended to give me back the money and so I should take it. Then she and I talked about what I should do. Cherokee women are not used to making this kind of decision, so she suggested that I visit with the colonel and ask his advice. So, that's what I'm going to do.

Finally, Col Loomis found time to talk with me, which taught me something – that I'm not the most important person in his life, and that's a position I'm unfamiliar and uncomfortable with. When I think back over my time with the Cherokees, I've always been important and sometimes even in charge. It was early afternoon when he could see me. I told him what Sookie and Wali planned to do and asked his advice about what I should do. He asked if I had any money and I told him I did. He said, "Well, that's one worry you won't have." Do you remember, Granny, that I told you that when we first came here he and Dog Shoot had talked a long time? Well, Dog Shoot told him my story and so he knew that I don't have any family near here.

When Col. Loomis told me that he thought I should go back to Alabama, I knew it was the right thing to do. I want to find out what's left of my family, and I want to see you, Granny. I know I want to be independent, but being with people who love me and understand me will make up for my not being in charge. I guess I want to be taken care of for a change. I talked to Col. Loomis about which route I should take. There are good roads to Fort Smith to the north and to Fort Jessup to the south. The northern route according to Col. Loomis will lead me across some mountains, but the crossing of the Mississippi River would likely be easier. The southern route is flatter and thus faster, but the Mississippi River will be wider and thus harder to cross. After thinking about it, I feel better about taking the southern, flatter route.

Anyway, I'm coming back home, and I mean really home – to Talledega. And I don't have to worry about money. It turns out that the letter Mr. Kimbrough sent had a gift of money in it for me. He told Col. Loomis to give me the money when the time was right. Of course, I wrote Mr. Kimbrough a long letter telling him all that had happened since we left Tallequah and my plans to go to Alabama. I thanked him for the money and posted the letter the next day.

So, big things are happening to me. I have plenty of clothes and plenty of money, so I'll catch the stagecoach to Fort Jessup as soon as Sookie and Wali and their children leave. Chooch, of course, is no longer a child and it is time for him to move on and find his family – for a lot of reasons, but I'll miss him and Sookie the most.

My Indian "family" left yesterday and left me to spend the night with Col. Loomis and Mrs. Loomis. The stagecoach to Fort Jessup leaves today. When the time came to leave, Col. Loomis gave me some additional money. He said he would sell my pony for me and he was sure that he could get his money back that way.

Although I am sad to be leaving, I am very excited about seeing you and what's left of my family in Alabama. So after all the adventures I've had – some good and some bad –I'm going back to where I started.

Part Three
Back to the Beginning

Entry 68

There are three people besides me making the trip to Birmingham. There is a man and his wife and their little boy. He's seven years old and that gives me the opportunity to practice my teaching on him. He likes to hear stories about Indians and other history, but I don't like to talk about that very much – living it once was enough. What I do when he starts asking to hear about "what happened," I guide him toward arithmetic. That's something else he likes, so it distracts him.

Something funny – or strange – happened on the first day (or "leg") of our stagecoach trip. After Andrew (the little boy) and I had gotten to know each other, we stopped at a stagecoach inn and ate. Then it was time to wash the dust off and get ready for bed. I was in a room by myself and the Thompson family (that's Andrew's mom and dad) occupied a larger room next to mine. Well, Andrew was fussy and cried shortly after we had all turned in. After being kept awake for a while, Mrs. Thompson knocked timidly on my door. When I opened the door, there she stood, holding Andrew's hand. He was snuffling and rubbing his eyes with his other hand. She apologized and said that they could not get him to settle down. I knelt down in front of him and asked what was wrong.

He let go of his mother's hand and rushed to me and knocked me over. Andrew and I were all in a heap. When we got straightened out, I asked him what was wrong. He asked me if he could please, please sleep with me. He said then he would be sure I would not leave during the night. Well, I had had experience with people leaving me, so I understood how he felt. I told him that he could sleep with me all the way to Birmingham. I didn't know what I was getting myself in for. I did not get another sound night's sleep as long as I shared my bed with that active seven-year-old.

Well, Granny, I didn't write in my journal every day on my way home. Every day on the stagecoach was long, hot, and very tiring. Every night was at a different inn with pretty good food and pretty bad beds. That's how my life went. In the little free time I had, I crocheted another pair of slippers because mine had gotten a little tight, as had my dresses and my real shoes. When I get to Talledega, I'll have some dressmaking to do.

The crossing of the Mississippi was not as bad as I expected. We crossed on a large flat-bottomed ferry. There were mules on each side of the river that pulled on ropes that were connected to pulleys. It was interesting, but by that time, I was too tired to pay attention

The trip from the Indian Territory to the Mississippi took nearly two weeks. I have mailed one real letter to you. I'll write again when we get across to Alabama, and will tell you when I will arrive in Talledega and you can arrange to meet the stagecoach. I hope you will be waiting for me at the stagecoach station. I'm so anxious to see you, Granny, that I welcome the time-consuming activities with Andrew. He's really a dear and refers to me as his big sister. That reminds me of when Dog Shoot called me his little sister.

Here we are in Birmingham, which turns out to be a pretty big town. The Thompsons asked me to go downtown with them. I figured they wanted me to keep an eye on Andrew, but that wasn't it at all. The Thompsons said they were so grateful for all the nights of solid sleep they had gotten and all the fun and learning Andrew had received that they wanted to try to repay me. They bought me an entire outfit, including a new pair of shoes. They were a little large, but the man who sold them to me said that I would "grow into them."

Entry 69

I am so sad, more so than when I lost anyone else who meant a lot to me. No one was at the station to meet me, so after waiting for a couple of hours, I made my way to Dr. Johnson's office. He is one of the few people in Talledega that I remember. I waited until he had finished his surgery. Then he ushered me into his office and gently told me that he was sorry to say that my granny had passed away only three weeks ago. Then, after I had taken that in, he told me that all the rest of my family had passed away, or had left the country except my uncle James and his family. They always lived at the family plantation and that isn't here in Talledega. Then Dr. Johnson took me home with him to Mrs. Johnson. She is one of the nicest people I have ever met. The Johnsons have three great children. The Johnsons must have told them that I was very sad because they didn't question me about my adventures, and that's something most children would have done. That night Mrs. Johnson took all my dirty clothes and gave them to the house slave to wash and iron. I slept in a small room on the third floor – what little I slept.

This morning after breakfast I carried my satchel with all my journals to the cemetery just south of town. I found out that it is called Oak Hill. I don't know if that is what it was called when we lived here because that isn't anything I would have been interested in at that age. I found your grave, Granny, and sat down next to it and read all my journals to you. That is what I had promised and I did it.

Then I talked to you just as if you could hear me. I guess writing in my journal has served as kind of talking things out. Putting things down on paper has served as a way of reasoning and of looking at all sides of a problem. My problem, and what I explained to you at the cemetery, is what I am going to do now. I have no family here and have never really known Uncle James and his children at the plantation. I can't expect Dr. and Mrs. Johnson to put me up for long, and I'm not old enough to get a job here in Talledega, and I am too young to live by myself anyway.

Another problem I thought I had turned out not to be a problem at all. At first I didn't know what to do with and about my journals. Then when I read them to you, Granny, I realized how much I had forgotten. So, without even thinking about it, I know I will keep my journals to let my children (if I ever have any) know the story of their mother's life and I will continue to write in them.

Entry 70

Later this evening I conferred with the Johnsons about my plight. They asked what I want to do, and I explained that I really don't know. What are my choices? I have no one to live with or to take care of me. Until I got here, I felt capable of taking care of myself. Maybe it comes from not living in a real town with plain people for so long. But now I am totally befuddled. If I stay here, I don't know what I'll do. If I were in Texas, I could at least find where my mother and father are buried and I could settle close to them.

Dr. Johnson told me that a Mr. Hawkins showed up in Talledega late in 1838 and told that there had been a massacre in Texas and that all the Killoughs had been killed. Well, obviously I had not been killed. I don't know if there were any others in my family who escaped. I am curious about that, but I don't dare let myself think about it. It would be too hard to take if anyone else had survived and then died before I found them. I am curious though about the property we had settled on. I overheard my Grandpa Killough telling his children that he owned the property. He had registered the deeds all proper and legal. I don't know if any of that land is mine. I think I need to go back to Texas, both to settle any legal questions there and to settle my mind that my family is really gone for good.

Dr. Johnson told me that he was aware of a young family with two small children who were planning to go to Texas, to Nacogdoches to be exact. Maybe I could hire out to take care of the children on the way in exchange for my passage. I'll have to think about that, but Dr. Johnson said I can stay with him and his wife for the next few days. During that time I can meet the Stantons – the couple going to Texas – and their children and make up my mind.

Entry 71

Today I met the Stantons and their children. They are a beautiful family. The children are Sarah, who is four and is a petite blond. Jacob is a typical six-year-old. He's always climbing trees, riding ponies, and playing cowboys and Indians. If they decide they want me, I think I will agree to go with them to Texas.

Later today I got word that the Stantons want me to accompany them on their journey. Until we leave, I'll live with the Stantons and help Mrs. S. get their clothes and everything ready. Before I leave the Johnsons, they want to give me a party that will be both a birthday and a going-away party. I lived with the Indians long enough that I had forgotten to celebrate my birthday. I'm 14 now, but I don't feel like having a party. There is just too much to be sad about. The Johnsons said they would make it a dinner instead of a party and they and everyone who once knew me or my family here in Talledega could say good-bye. It's kinda strange that I may never have a party of my own and yet I turned this one down.

The morning after the dinner party I slept late – a real luxury. When I did get up, all my clothes were clean, pressed, and packed into a portmanteau – a gift from the Johnsons. After the noonday meal, I went over to the Stantons and moved in there. I'll have to find a way to repay the Johnsons for their hospitality and their help.

Life at the Stantons is hectic, what with packing, with extra items to be given away, and other supplies to be bought. Of course, the slaves do all the work, but they need close supervision and instruction. The children are delightful. They are so excited they jump around, scream, and generally wear themselves out. Every afternoon they rest, as does the entire household. I read to the children or tell them stories until they fall asleep.

Each night at supper, the Stantons report to each other what they have accomplished that day. They ask the children what they learned or had done that day. They are such smart, dear children, and they make me look good. They just soak up every bit of information they see or hear. That tells me a couple of things. First, I need to be careful what I say around them, and second, I need to make sure they understand what they hear. One day I was helping one of the house slaves go through some items that would be left behind when I said to the slave that little pitchers have big ears. Of course, the slave knew what I meant and became more guarded in her talk.

Later, at supper, Jacob was looking around the table curiously. When his daddy asked what in the world he was looking for, he looked at me and said, "But Hannah, I don't see any ears." I explained to him what I meant and the entire family had a big laugh.

Entry 72

Today Mr. Stanton had a wagon delivered to the house. He sent a message by the boy who delivered it that we would need to plan the packing of this wagon with household goods and currently unneeded clothes. Mrs. S. would not let us actually load anything into the wagon yet. That night when Mr. Stanton got home, Mrs. S. asked him exactly what his plan was. According to Mr. Stanton, one large covered wagon will carry beds, furniture, cookware, etc. A second, and smaller wagon would be for the family to ride in during the day and more or less live out of, and to sleep in at night.

Mrs. S. brought up the subject of pets. Sarah would be allowed to take one cat and Jacob could take his little dog. Jacob brought up the subject of where his favorite slaves, Sadie and Tom, would ride and sleep. Mrs. S. gently told Jacob that they would sell all their slaves before they left and would have to "do" for themselves until they got to Nacogdoches, where they would have to buy new slaves. Well, that set both children off crying. When Sadie came into the room to see what was wrong, both Sarah and Jacob ran to her and wrapped their arms around her legs and wailed about leaving her behind. Then this set her off crying and Mr. Stanton ordered Sadie, the two children, and even me, to leave the room. When we got to their room, it took all Sadie and I could do to quiet them down. Finally, when the children had tired themselves out with crying, they fell asleep. Sadie and I moved out into the hallway and sat down on the top of the stairs.

That is where Mrs. S. found us a little later. Sadie told her that although she loved the two children, there was no way she would leave her family and friends and go to Texas. I promised Sadie that I would love and take good care of the children until I had to leave them in Nacogdoches. Then we all went on to bed.

Entry 73

This morning Mr. Stanton said that his wife had a headache and that Sadie and I would have to direct the men in loading the large wagon. After breakfast, we set the men to work. The children were excited and tried to help. Of course, they got in the way more than they helped, but everyone treated them kindly. Tonight Mr. Stanton brought home the small wagon that would be our home for the next three months. Mrs. S. came down to supper and said that we would load the small wagon tomorrow. Then when Mr. Stanton gets home, he can see how much we have left and decide whether we will need one more small wagon.

Today we loaded the things we will need on the trip.

Tonight Mr. and Mrs. Stanton sat down and tried to make a list of additional things to put in another small wagon. When they were through, the children went to bed. By the time I got back downstairs, they had decided not to get a third wagon. Mr. Stanton is a lawyer and will make enough money at his new firm in Nacogdoches to buy all they need.

The things that are left here Mrs. S. will give to Sadie and will write a letter saying that the items were given to her and were not stolen. Mr. Stanton has talked to Dr. Johnson and he will buy Sadie and Tom. That's a real relief to both the Stantons. So now it's final: we leave for Texas in two days.

Entry 74

I didn't write in my journal the last two days because, first of all, we were too busy, and secondly, too nervous.

Everybody is getting on everybody else's nerves. But, today we left. Mr. Stanton planned for us to go west and meet up with some other wagons about five miles out of town. It was about time for the mid-day meal when we found the other wagons, so we had a light meal and visited with the people we would be spending the next three months with. There are six other children besides the Stantons two. So, with Mr. Stanton's permission, I asked their mother if they would like to come to our little school every day. Their mother was pleased for the three youngest children to attend school, but she said the older three were too rowdy and that she would keep them with her. She thanked me and called me a "God-send." Then we moved on west until it was time to stop for the day. When we made camp, the women put their supper food together and made a big pot of stew, which we all shared. I showed the women how to bake (cornbread in this case) in a Dutch oven, and it was good.

It seems as if most of the women in our group were used to having slaves do all the work for them. My time with the Cherokees taught me to do many of the things the slaves would have done. I'm especially glad that Sookie took the time to teach me so many things. Mrs. Stanton warned me not to let the women treat me like a slave, to remember that I was hired to teach the Stanton children and to take care of them. She did agree that I could show the women how to do certain things, such as cook, but that was all, and I was not to do their work for them.

Since we have no way of keeping meat, the men go out very early and try to shoot a deer or bear or something. Then the women (with a lot of instruction from me) dress the animal and we have it for dinner and supper. We have been able to bring enough salt with us to preserve the meat as long as we need to. I have not told Mrs. S. that I know how to get salt out of rain water. We aren't in one spot long enough to make it anyway.

Entry 75

We had a strange experience today. One of the families in our little group had their old grandmother traveling with them. She had been old, tired, and kinda sick when we left Talledega, and she died in the night last night. So today we didn't move at all. The men dug a grave while the women washed and dressed the body. I wondered what they would use for a coffin, but a couple of the men cut down a pine tree and made planks out of it and then made a coffin. It was late afternoon when we had the actual burial. It was a sad thing with each of the grown-ups saying something. Since I am about half grown up, they expected me to say something, so I said, "Rest in peace."

We had a meal and went to bed early. This gives me time to write in my journal. I lay awake a long time, wondering how the family would ever find their grandma's grave later. We are not in a town, or even near one so far as I know, so if they want to visit her grave, how will they ever find it? I guess getting older has not made me any less curious.

We got back to our regular routine today. After breakfast, we got on our journey again. We had our usual school lessons in the morning and then stopped for our mid-day meal. This usually consists of biscuits or cornbread left from the previous day's supper. The women make gravy and we will eat some left-over meat. Sometimes it will be fried squirrel or some other fried meat. Sometimes we have venison (deer meat) and the men talk about killing a bear, but it hasn't happened yet. There is always milk from the cows that one family herds along in front of the wagons. We have plenty of eggs and that's kinda funny.

One woman has about a dozen hens and she treats them like babies. She lets them out in the morning and they keep up with us, all the while she is talking to them, calling them "girls." Then she loads them into her wagon and feeds them. They ride in the wagon all afternoon and they seem to know that it is time for them to lay eggs. By the next morning, we have plenty of eggs for breakfast and some days there are enough for the women to use in cooking supper that night.

We usually stop for the night while there are at least a couple of hours of daylight left. Sometimes someone will bake something special in the Dutch oven while others cook the meat and whatever else we are going to eat. Everyone has brought along a lot of food that won't spoil, like potatoes, turnips, carrots, onions, etc. We all eat together every meal. The men decided that the food would last longer that way. I have also noticed that we are closer to each other because of sharing our meals. The whole experience is kinda fun. The children sure think so, and I still have enough kid in me that I think so, too.

Entry 76

We've been traveling a couple of weeks now. I no longer worry about what day it is. This is probably because we are never very far from a town, and we can find out the date if we really need to know. Also, maybe some of the Indians' attitude wore off on me. One thing that I have noticed, too, is the weather. It has been mostly dry. It's funny how you think about the weather depending on what you're doing. If we were trying to farm, we would probably worry more about it than we do traveling. Now rain just makes the trail muddy and slow, and the streams we have to cross are wider than we would like. One other thing, when the weather is good, the men and boys usually sleep on the ground under the wagons, while the women and girls sleep in them.

Today was a very good day. One of the hens (girls) died last night and Mrs. Broaddus said she died of old age and the stress of the journey, so we could eat her and not run the risk of getting sick. The chickens belong to Mrs. Broaddus, so I guess she knows what she is talking about.

Fried chicken is my favorite thing to eat, but chicken and dumplings are good too. Also, that goes a lot farther than fried, so that's what we decided to have. While we were traveling today, Mrs. Broaddus plucked the chicken and cut it into small pieces. We stopped for the day near a running stream, so we filled the Dutch oven with water and put the chicken pieces in it to boil.

There are four people in the Broaddus family. Mr. Broaddus drives the wagon. It was his sister who died and was buried a couple of days ago. His and Mrs. Broaddus' son and daughter-in-law are with them. They haven't been married long and don't have any children. They remind me of Elizabeth and Kias.

The other family besides the Broaddus's and the Stantons are the Akers. Mrs. Akers is large and loud and rather rough, while Mr. Akers is small and always defers to his wife, whom he calls Mother. They have six children, two boys and a girl who do not come to school and two girls and a boy who do. The three oldest are the ones that Mrs. Akers said were too wild to behave in school. That just leaves the Stantons and their two children and me.

So supper that night had to feed seventeen people – with just one old, skinny chicken. The way that problem was solved was that everyone got one little bite of chicken, some broth and all the dumplings they wanted. Of course, there were vegetables, milk, and even a dessert. All-in-all nobody went away hungry and everybody agreed that it was the best meal we had to date.

We continued our travels today. Mr. Broaddus (the younger) says we are only a couple of days from the Mississippi River

Entry 77

So, here we are at the Mississippi River again. As we took our turns crossing, I sat to the side, wrote a little in this book, and mostly thought back over the last six years. I thought about all the rivers I had crossed and what each crossing brought me to. It would have been easy to think about all the things and especially people I have lost, but that way leads to sadness and despair. I learned long ago not to think of things that will make me sad.

Anyway here we are with just the Louisiana Territory and a little bit of Texas to cross to get to Nacogdoches. We talk about our parting our ways in Nacogdoches. This upsets the children, so I tell the children stories (made up, of course) about what lies ahead. I keep the focus on them because I am actually scared of what my future holds.

We continue our lessons every morning. I try to remember what all Elizabeth taught and pass that along to my students. They seem to love to learn and I hope that when we reach Nacogdoches, they will move into the classes they would have been in if they had been attending a regular school.

It's been nearly two weeks since we crossed the Mississippi and we are nearly to Nacogdoches. We are going to have a final supper together tonight and then tomorrow enter Nacogdoches and go our separate ways. During the evening the Akers came to me and tried to pay me for teaching their children. I did not want to take their money, so I sent them to see the Stantons since I have been working for them and they are the ones who let the other children sit in on their children's lessons.

Later that night, both Mr. and Mrs. Stanton came to find me. They told me how much I had meant to them and to the children. Of course I said that they had been more than kind to me. When I needed a way to get to Texas, they provided it and even paid me. It seems as if I have gained more from our association than they have.

Entry 78

After our last night together, we parted ways this morning. I took my money and went to the livery stable. There I made a deal to buy a pony and the tack for it. This left me with a little money, so I had to figure out what kind of food to buy for my trip. The liveryman said that I could make it in three days. Of course, he doesn't know I have been riding for several years and I am sure I will be there in two days at the most. The problem will come when I get there. I have no idea what awaits me there.

The man at the livery stable said there is a direct road I can take. It is called the Neches-Saline Road. Both of those names mean something to me, so I'm sure it will take me right where I want to go. Some of the men sitting around the livery stable said that a new town, called Larissa, had been incorporated by the county government. This area is part of Nacogdoches County. Before I leave, I'll go to the county courthouse here in Nacogdoches and see what I can find out about that area.

A really nice man at the courthouse read through some records and then ushered me into a small room where we could talk uninterrupted. He told me that a Nathaniel Killough had petitioned the court to grant him title to all the land the Killough family lost in the massacre plus such money as the household goods and crops were worth. The man told me that the Nacogdoches Commissioners' Court endorsed the petition and sent it on to the Supreme Court of Texas in Austin. It was his understanding that the Supreme Court had granted the petition. He also said that there was a document in the works to make Texas a state of the United States of America. If that happens, and he is sure that it will, all petitions granted by the courts of Texas will be valid in the United States.

If all this is true, at least one of my relatives, Uncle Nathaniel, survived. That makes me more anxious than ever to get back to our (the Killough) land.

When I got back to the livery stable, the stagecoach had just pulled up. I asked that my pony be saddled up for my journey. The man who owns the stable came over to talk to me. He told me that the stagecoach is going the same way as I was and that the driver would be glad to tie my pony to the stage and let me ride inside. The stage is going to Skin Tight today and will spend the night there. Then I can ride my pony on to Larissa from there. The stagecoach will veer toward the northeast on its way to Shreveport, Louisiana. I said I would just as soon ride my pony all the way. The men standing around warned me of all sorts of dangers on the road. I hesitated to tell them all I had been through since the age of eight. Somehow I didn't want to share my story with strangers, so I finally agreed to their plans for me.

They all contributed some money and bought me a ticket to Skin Tight. When I started to tell them that I had money of my own to pay my way, the livery owner interrupted me and took me aside. He said to never ever let on that I had any money He said you never know who might steal your money, and maybe even your life. I agreed and thanked all the men warmly for their generosity. About that time, the owner of a nearby eating establishment brought box dinners for everyone on the stage and again the men from the livery stable insisted on buying my dinner. I was really glad to leave for a couple of reasons. First, I'm tall for my age and I guess I look older than I am and I got the feeling that some of the men seemed to think that I am prime marrying age. Also, I am eager to get on my way to Larissa, plus, I was so hungry by this time that food was all I could think about. My pony had been fed at the livery stable, so he was o.k.

Entry 79

So the stagecoach pulled out and the six passengers (including me) ate pieces of cold fried chicken, biscuits, pickles, corn on the cob, milk, etc. Although it wasn't getting dark yet, after about four hours on the road, we arrived at Skin Tight. A Mr. and Mrs. Cleaver met the stage and urged us to come into their big house and make ourselves at home. Mister Cleaver went out with the stage driver to show him where the horses would be stabled and to put my pony up for the night.

Meanwhile Mrs. Cleaver showed us where we would sleep. The driver and the three male passengers will sleep in one large room while the three women passengers (including me) will share another bedroom that had three feather beds! Then it was time to eat. The Cleavers' household help were really good cooks. After supper we all turned in early. I had not been in such a soft, comfortable bed since Talledega, and it didn't take but a minute for me to fall asleep.

Early the next morning, as soon as breakfast was over, the stagecoach and its five passengers left for Shreveport.

As Mr. Cleaver was saddling my pony and tying my carpetbag and small portmanteau to the saddle, we began talking. He asked where I was going and if I would be met there. When I said I was going to Larissa, he said he had a friend there by the name of Nathaniel Killough. I was flabbergasted and without thinking, said, "You know Uncle Nathaniel?" That shocked him and he stammered, "How is that? I thought all the rest of the Killoughs were dead."

It dawned on me that I had been keeping my story more or less a secret – and I don't know why. Mr. Cleaver was so very kind that I trusted him with a little bit of my story. I told him that my last name was Williams, but my mother had been a Killough before she married. Mr. Cleaver looked at me strangely and said, "I'll not intrude on your privacy, but I do insist on riding part of the way with you – not that I don't think you can look after yourself."

I made a little curtsy and told him that I would be honored to have such a noble traveling companion. He laughed and saddled his own horse and a pack mule and tied my bags on the mule. We stopped by his house for him to tell Mrs. Cleaver where he was going, and then we were off on the last leg of my journey.

Entry 80

The ride to Larissa was uneventful but rather tiring. A few miles short of my destination, we stopped at the home of one of Mr. Cleaver's friends. We had a light meal with them and Mr. Cleaver stayed to talk business and to spend the night. Then he planned to return home the next day. He gave me directions and said I should be there in an hour at the least.

I must admit that it was all I could to keep from running my poor little pony all the way. Now that I know that Uncle Nathaniel is still in the area – although there was no town the last time I was there – I can hardly wait to see him. Mr. Cleaver said he didn't know exactly where Uncle Nathaniel lived, but he is a rather prominent person, so it won't be hard to find him.

Something really strange happened as I neared Larissa. Where I had been so eager to see Uncle Nathaniel, the closer I got, the more I seemed to hang back. Instead of going straight into the town, I headed out to where our cabins were. When I got to the location, there were a few rough tombstones. On some of them was the name "Killough" carved in the stone. I sat down in the midst of them and let myself cry. I cried for my family; for my mother and daddy and the rest of my family, for all the people I have loved and have lost – Mr. Benge, Duwali, and dear, sweet Dog Shoot, and maybe most of all for the childhood I never had.

As I cried, a little black and brown fiest dog crept up to me. He reminded me so much of my little cousin Billy's dog that I said, "What is your name? Is it Spotty?" That was Billy's dog's name. I swear he acted like he recognized that name. The dog finally ran off and I prepared myself to go into town and try to find Uncle Nathaniel.

Entry 81

The "town" of Larissa is not much of a town, at least not compared to Nacogdoches. There are a few retail establishments, a church, a school, and several houses. It reminds me a little of Tallequah in the Indian Territory. The first store I came to was a great deal like Mr. K's in Tallequah. It even had a post office section in one corner. There were several people (mostly men) milling around. They seemed excited about something and were talking among themselves until I came in. Suddenly everyone fell silent and seemed to be watching me intently. The store-keeper, a Mr. Brown, came over to me and asked if he could help me. I told him that I was looking for a Mr. Nathaniel Killough. The customers began whispering again and Mr. Brown said that Mr. Nathaniel had been in the store not fifteen minutes ago, but that the boy visiting him had come in and told him some story and that Mr. Nathaniel left with him. I asked where I might find his house. The people in the store gave me directions and said to wait at Mr. Nathaniel's and they would find him and tell him that a young lady awaited him at home.

As I left the store, two or three men ran out and got on their horses and rode off in different directions. As it turned out, they went to find Uncle Nathaniel to tell him that he had company. I went on to Uncle Nathaniel's house. It was an impressive two-storey house with a female slave who seemed to be in charge. She showed me to the parlor, and I sat down to wait.

After about 20 minutes – there was a beautiful mantle clock in the parlor – I heard horses approaching. In a couple of minutes, first the little fiest from the grave sites came bounding into the room. I sat on the floor and held him in my lap until a tall man walked in. We just looked at each other for a period of time – it was definitely Uncle Nathaniel. I jumped up and cried out, "Uncle Nathaniel" at the same time that he said, "Hannah Grace!" We hugged and laughed and cried. He told me that I looked like my mother when she was my age, even more so than Elizabeth did. After we had composed ourselves, he turned to the doorway and said, "Well, boy, come meet your cousin." A little boy about seven years old shyly sidled into the room. The little dog ran up to him and proceeded to jump up and down on him. I said, "Are you really Billy, and is this Spotty?" He said, "Yessum." I laughed and said, "I'm not a ma'am; I'm your cousin – that means that I'm part of your family."

About that time, the girl announced that supper was ready. Supper took a long time, as Uncle Nathaniel told me the story of the massacre as he knew it. I promised to let him read my journals tonight.

Part of what he told me was really upsetting. Both of my parents survived the massacre only to be taken by consumption just a couple of years back. Tomorrow Uncle Nathaniel will take me to see their graves and the next day Aunt Jane will be here to pick up Billy, who is just visiting. Aunt Jane has remarried and lives nearby.

After supper, I gave all my journals to Uncle Nathaniel to read and I retired to the guest room.

I guess I'll stay here in Larissa. Uncle Nathaniel says I will never want for anything. I hesitate to tell him that I've never experienced want for anything, except family. Of course, I can't feel sorry for myself for long – that's just not my nature. I know that all the experiences I've had –both good and bad – have made me the person I am today, and I think I like who I am.

The End

CPSIA information can be obtained at www.ICGtesting.com
Printed in the USA
LVOW100524250313

325797LV00004B/13/P